FIRSTBORN ACADEMY

SHADOW REAPER

ISLA FROST

Copyright © 2020 by Isla Frost
All rights reserved.

Published by JFP Trust
2020 First Print Edition

ISBN: 978 0 6482532 9 7

www.islafrost.com

CHAPTER ONE

My hand trailed over the ornate wood paneling of the sentient manor that had become a second home to me in the past six months. A second home for a second version of myself perhaps. So much had happened…

But today we would leave this home too.

We would travel through a series of magic gateways to join the other walker and human hollows at the war front. A *series* of gateways over shorter and shorter distances to minimize the risk of the enemy using those same gateways to advance into new, unguarded territory. And then we would come face-to-face with the nightmare in the light of day.

The nightmare that had gone unstopped for 150 years. The nightmare that had devoured the life force from one world and was now well on its way to devouring this one.

"I think I'm going to miss you, Millicent," I murmured.

The floorboards thrummed under my feet in a purring sort of agreement, and a unicorn on the wallpaper tossed its head in a way that might pass as a nod.

The manor's custodian, on the other hand, would not be sad to see us go. Emptying the academy of its students would greatly reduce the staff's workload for the next six months until the following intake. The two-headed creature was holding Millicent's front door wide open (an entirely unnecessary task since Millicent was perfectly capable of doing so herself) in a clear invitation for us to see ourselves out to the lawn for departure.

Glenn, the usually surly head on the right, was smiling what might have been the least mean-spirited smile I'd ever seen on his delicately tapered snout. He said something to Glennys—who was very literally his better half—and she leaned her head against his in what could only be described as long-suffering affection. Wow. If I didn't find it so hard to wrap my head around, I might've thought Glenn had said something *nice*.

I turned to my friends. As much as I would miss Millicent, I was far from alone.

How different this departure would be from when I'd stepped through the runegate six months ago. Ameline, my warm and wonderful best friend since forever, was still beside me, but other friends had been added to that number. First Bryn, a fearless girl with a heart of fire and an unhealthy penchant for trouble, and more hesitantly, cautiously, uneasily, Theus and Lirielle too.

Theus was the walker who'd changed my mind about walkerkind. A feat I would've once thought impossible. And now that I *had* realized walkers were not the enemy, my feelings for him had only grown more complicated. Lirielle was strange, even by walker standards, but lovable in the way of stray cats and eccentric aunts with very sharp claws (or swords in her case) and a knack for glimpsing the future.

Plus there was Ameline's pygmy griffin friend Griff. He was magnificence in miniature now, his plumage golden to match Ameline's hair, his cat coat sleek and spotted over his muscled haunches, and his avian gaze fierce and intelligent.

Ameline had tried to convince him to stay here in the forest where he'd be safer, but he'd adamantly refused. She claimed it was because he'd acquired a taste for smoked fish, but I thought he'd just fallen in love with Ameline's gentle charm the way pretty much everyone did.

Typical, said a voice in my head in an all-too-familiar tone of complaint.

I glanced down at my sheathed sword and with-held a sigh. Not that my restraint did much good since Gus could read my mind when the mood struck

3

him, which I suspected was more often than he let on. That "feature" was supposed to help us work as one in battle, but I considered it more of a defect.

You count the fish-guzzling featherhead among your companions, but your sword, who has protected you, defended you, even gone against his religion and killed *for you, doesn't warrant a spared thought?*

"Oh, Gus dear," I crooned. "I had no idea you aspired to be numbered among my friends."

He growled. *Friend, no. That would be like a majestic dragon befriending a tapeworm. The tapeworm being you in this analogy, you understand. But I deserve to be admired, appreciated, revered. That sort of thing.*

"I do appreciate you," I soothed. "You're an inestimably valuable pain in my neck. And if I could wiggle my way through your majestic digestive tract and into your heart, I totally would."

He snorted, but I thought he sounded at least a little mollified. Probably because he'd found another opportunity to insult me rather than because he cared a whit what I thought.

So I didn't spare him any further headspace as I walked with my friends to the waiting gateway.

Yes, it was different this time.

Instead of stepping into the unknown, I knew exactly where I was going and why. Instead of a self-assigned mission to tear down the Agreement between walkers and humans, I was determined to use the power woken in me to save both our peoples. To save the world.

My horizons were far broader than the sheltered life I'd led in the ruins of Los Angeles, surrounded by my community of one species, one version of history, and their small everyday concerns.

Oh yes, the academy had changed me. Had empowered me, humbled me, trained me, and set me up for a victory or fall far greater than I'd ever dreamed of.

And I'd already possessed dreams larger than anyone I knew.

The familiar grass of the manor's grounds flattened beneath my weight for probably the last time as we approached the magical gateway. How casual a thing it was now to translocate, to step through the fabric of our world and arrive in a new place.

With Bryn's and Ameline's hands gripping mine, we braced for the skin-crawling static and stepped into our future.

This time I knew the who, what, where, and why.

The only questions remaining were how on earth could we pull off the inconceivable? And if victory *was* possible, how many of us would survive to see it?

CHAPTER TWO

Our new home was to be nothing like the old.

Instead of pristine lawn and flourishing flower beds hemmed all around by a dangerous forest swarming with life, desolation stretched as far as the eye could see.

We stood atop a bare brown mound that must have once been part of rolling green hills, and below us was a sweeping vista of more bare brown ground. The only break in this monotonous landscape was the military base itself. Like an oasis in the desert, except this land should never have been comparable to a desert.

The sun beat down overhead, and there was nothing to protect us or the barren earth from its glare. The faint scent of smoke carried to us on the inadequate breeze, and the sky seemed impossibly vast without trees or buildings to frame it.

As we'd neared our destination, our classmates had been split into smaller groups and whisked to different locations. Now there were only seventeen of us left. But that number included each of my friends. Plus a few walkers who were decidedly *not*.

What a shame Ellbereth and her staunchest crony hadn't been whisked to a different location. Like a nice, dank, sulfurous cave where they could polish her horns and stay far away from me. Her life and mine were irreversibly bound, and while she'd stopped trying to kill me because that would necessitate her own death, her loathing had increased with every day she'd failed to make me pay for that fact.

The seventeen of us stepped through a final short-distance gateway. Suddenly, instead of looking down on the base from one of the brown hills, we were nose to nose with the fringe of greenery that surrounded the base.

Professor Cricklewood, who had broken away from the other academy teachers to escort us through these last few gateways, thumped his walking staff into the dirt for our attention.

"You've all come a long way from the beetle-brained, pigeon-livered, sniveling snot urchins that first dragged themselves onto my training ground." His gaze touched each of us but rested a fraction longer on me. "So try not to get yourselves killed in your first week here, all right?"

That speech was positively gushy for the cranky

old professor. He stepped back through the gateway and winked out of sight.

Someone cleared their throat, and we turned to face a slender young man who was leaning on a nearby building, one elbow propped against the timber wall. Carefully styled dirty-blond curls, bright gray eyes, and a full mouth angled with mischief gave the walker a jaunty, almost foppish air.

Not what I expected from a military base. Especially after encountering my old friend Fletcher and seeing the changes the war had wrought in him.

The walker lifted his hand in a bastardization of a salute and a wave. "Welcome to hell," he said cheerfully. "I'm Silvyr of the thirty-first intake, and I've been assigned the dubious privilege of being your tour guide."

Despite his words, he didn't seem to mind the duty. After a brief exchange of introductions—in which his eyes lingered long enough to indicate he knew I was the girl with "the magic of the enemy" but not how he felt about that—he led us around the grounds.

Hell proved to be an overstatement.

The base setup was pleasant enough in a functional, nondescript sort of way. The buildings were unmemorable, temporary, not the usual walker style. And they lacked the rich sense of history imbued in Millicent, not to mention her character. The only sign of sentience I witnessed was the self-opening doors.

But the beds looked soft, and each unit in the rows of sleeping quarters boasted its own washroom with something that resembled toilets and showers—even though there was a distinct lack of plumbing. Shared areas included a mess hall and several under-cover outdoor areas for off-duty armsmen.

A few of those off-duty walkers and firstborns milled about, some ignoring our group, others greeting Silvyr or calling a welcome to the newbies. Not a single one of them called me an abomination as I passed or leveled glares of loathing my way.

Maybe they just didn't know who I was yet.

"All our bases are limited to three hundred armsmen to dilute the natural regeneration effect of having a bunch of walkers residing in one place," Silvyr was explaining. "We don't want any of our sites to regrow so much life as to present a tempting morsel for the Malus. Ambushes in the middle of the night aren't a lot of fun. Plus having troops spread around the perimeter shaves seconds off response times since we're limited to short-distance translocation, and gate-waying *through* the Malus is too dangerous."

He showed us the "eatery"—a kind of walk-in larder well stocked with fresh bread and fruit and huge bowls of ready-made meals under the same magical preserving covers they used at the academy.

"It's a serve-yourself system. All meals and freshly laundered uniforms and bedding are translocated in from the capital so that when you're off duty, you're able to rest and do what you need to in order to keep yourselves sane." Silvyr's full lips twisted into a sardonic half smile. "Or at least what passes for sane around here. Never fear, the bar is pretty low."

We exited the eatery and passed another shared under-cover area. Except this one was splattered all over with black gunk.

"Don't mind the mess. That's from Blob Blast, a popular form of stress relief. You'll doubtless see it later."

He didn't elaborate, just led us onward to a large storeroom. It was unlocked and unguarded.

"Uniforms and shield nets are in here. The adjacent building houses weapon-maintenance supplies and expendables like arrows, crossbow bolts, concealers, and explosives. The uniforms are self-altering, so grab a couple of sets each and I'll run through the use of your shield nets."

We did as we were bid. The uniforms felt sturdier than our academy clothing but were in the same colors, midnight blues and blacks. Close-fitting long sleeves and pants. No damned tie, thank goodness. The most significant difference was an armored vest that went overtop. Glimmering gold and incredibly light, it was like otherworldly chain mail in a design inspired by forest leaves and dragon scales.

The beauty of it made you want to stand up straight, instilling a sense of gravitas, significance, pride. The idea that in donning this uniform, we were joining something larger than ourselves. Something that had existed before we were born. Something millions of lives were depending on. Something important.

The shield nets were black half spheres the size of an orange that attached to our belts behind our hip. Which hip depended on our weapon of choice and which hand we were likely to have free.

Silvyr held one up. "This unassuming little piece of equipment is essential to your continued survival, so listen carefully. You would have learned about the Malus's vortex power in class, but until you live through it, *if* you live through it, you have no idea how stars-damned awful it is. When the Malus starts its temper tantrum, you have about two seconds to get to the ground and deploy your shield net. Those that fail to do this have about a one in fifteen chance of making it out alive and one in fifty of making it back sane, so don't mess around. If you hear a low hissing wail or if you see the earth begin to tremble or your unit commander gives the order, get your ass on the ground. Even if you have to fling away your weapon, risk a blow from an opponent, or dive into a patch of still-burning terrain to do it."

Silvyr strapped the half sphere to his own belt and demonstrated. Somehow he made a headlong dive to the dirt look graceful, and when the shield net deployed, a light web sprang from the device and covered him in less time than it took to blink.

From beneath the net, Silvyr said, "The webbing anchors you to the ground and hardens to protect you from flying debris and creatures controlled by the Malus. Wait for your unit commander's order before you release yourself."

The net withdrew into the sphere, and Silvyr stood and dusted himself off. "Now it's your turn. When I whistle, get to the ground as fast as possible and deploy your shield net. Last to do so gets to clean the common areas for a week."

Silvyr whistled. We dove. Both my arms wanted to break my fall, but I forced my left to stay on the shield net and pressed it as soon as I thought I was close enough. The webbing was partially transparent, so I could see someone hadn't been so lucky. They'd deployed theirs too soon and were now stumbling around tightly bound in the net.

At least that meant I wasn't last.

"I've seen worse," Silvyr said. "But three of you would've died. Everyone get up, and any time I whistle throughout the rest of your induction, same rules apply. That way the losers will have some help cleaning."

He slipped an exquisitely sculpted tiny metal lizard from his pocket and held it up, reminding me of the animated dragon lock and, less fondly, of the bloodjewel beetles. "These are how units communicate with each other and receive new orders from the command station when you're on the field. For some reason no one remembers, they're known as squeakers."

He lifted the golden figurine to the side of his head. The lizard promptly curled itself around his outer ear and positioned its tiny maw to speak directly into his ear canal.

Silvyr angled his head so everyone could see. "The squeaker will relay in near perfect imitation anything anyone in your unit says as well as anything headquarters wants you to hear. They don't relay other noises. You'll receive one once you've been assigned to your new unit.

"There's no need to wear them when you're off duty. We have a horrendous screeching alarm that will wake you so fast you'll bite your tongue if the base is under attack or all units are needed in an emergency. If that happens, drop what you're doing, gear up, and get your butts as fast as possible to the largest common area, the one with the Blob Blast mess."

Silvyr whistled. I wasted half a second remembering what that meant, then dove to the ground, smacked my chin in the dirt, and deployed my shield net. Somehow I still wasn't last.

Silvyr was grinning when we climbed back up. "Now I know why some people like command. This is sort of fun."

Bryn rolled her eyes, but since she'd been the first one to hit the ground, I suspected she was feeling pretty pleased with herself. To be fair, she had less distance to travel.

I did not point this out to her.

Griff had wisely departed from Ameline's shoulder and was perched on a rooftop, watching the crazy humans and walkers do their crazy things. Unlike Gus, *he* refrained from commenting.

I agree with the walker fellow. This is kind of fun. I wonder if I can mimic his whistle in your head...

"Don't you *dare*," I growled.

Gus snickered.

Finding Silvyr's eyes on me, I held back my threats for later. Or maybe if I was lucky, Gus would do the courtesy of plucking them from my mind.

"Right, we've talked a lot about your off-duty time, but I'll briefly run through what they sent you here for other than sleeping and eating and rolling in the dirt."

A few of us snorted appreciatively.

"You'll soon find out that this war is like nothing in the history books. We have two opposing forces that have to exert tremendous amounts of effort just to cause minimal harm to the other. Which ultimately means a lot of hard work with little to show for it. Unfortunately, the Malus doesn't have to kill our armsmen for us to lose. So it's a war we've been gradually losing for 150 years."

There was no humor on Silvyr's face now.

"Our forces are divided into units of twelve

because we're spread thin and need to be agile and swift to respond to changing conditions. That said, you'll often work with multiple other units on a given mission.

"Our chain of command is pretty flat, with the lord general on top, his various aides next, followed by field commanders, unit commanders, and then general armsmen—that's you. So your job is to perform any order you're given. Newbies normally shadow another unit for a few months before forming up into teams of their own. But I understand there are special circumstances around this year's wildcard, which the relevant people will be filled in on later."

Silvyr's lively face offered no clues what those special circumstances might be, and I felt my stomach tighten. Special circumstances could mean anything.

"Once you've been assigned to a unit, your primary duties will be one of five tasks. The first is blazer duty—that's burning large swathes of land to reduce the life force the Malus can take from a given area. It also aids in influencing the direction and speed of its advance.

"Evac duty works in tandem with the first, evacuating the area of any living being that is willing and able to leave.

"Watch duty takes more man power than anything else. We maintain twenty-four-hour surveillance around the perimeter of the Malus, which is currently the size of a small country. Much like what used to be Germany for those of you that means something to.

"Strike duty is dangerous but straightforward. Essentially you go wherever you're needed to defend other troops or those vulnerable in the line of the Malus's advance.

"The final primary task you might find yourself assigned to is void duty. Only walkers can open gateways of course, but those walkers need defending, so units still operate as complete teams. You would've learned at the academy that opening a giant gateway into the void between worlds can discourage the Malus from advancing toward a highly populated area or stop a charge in its tracks. In the early days, we even destroyed sections of the Malus by maneuvering them into the void. Until it wised up to that tactic. But void gateways remain useful for temporary shielding and for manipulating the direction of the Malus.

"Enough of that. You'll learn a great deal more from shadowing an experienced unit than listening to me. Do you have any questions?"

We didn't. We'd already been taught this stuff at the academy, though it had never felt as real as it did now. And I knew none of those tactics held the answers I was seeking. Answers on how to *defeat* the Malus rather than merely slow it down.

"Great. Then who wants to get a sneak peek of the enemy?"

Silvyr asked this like he was asking a bunch of kids

Who wants cake? and expecting the equivalent response. But all he received was stiff nods.

He looked faintly disappointed.

"Usually you just get a boring visual gateway tour, but I know someone in the Fleetfox unit who's befriended a herd of stormriders, so I have a special treat for you."

On cue, a gateway rippled into existence and the first stormrider stepped through.

CHAPTER THREE

Thunder reverberated across the clear sky, and the hair on my arms stood to attention in the suddenly electrically charged air.

Professor Wilverness had once explained how millennia ago the worlds were close together and creatures occasionally crossed between them, which was why so many of our mythical creatures had turned out to have a basis in reality.

The first stormrider to step through the gateway looked altogether like a unicorn out of legend. A coat of purest white, eyes like a summer sky and bright with a wild intelligence, and a long, flowing mane dancing on a breeze that hadn't existed a moment ago. Except lightning flickered over its delicate but wickedly tapered horn, and overhead, a storm was rolling in with impossible swiftness.

I was transfixed. The creature's beauty awaking a

fierce awe and longing that I felt as an ache in my chest. And more stormriders were stepping through, their soft coats bathed in light as if the sun shone behind them, their colors ranging like the clouds from bright white to dark gray.

Silvyr rushed around and gave us each a handful of blush-pink gladberries along with rapid instructions.

"Stand very still, keep your eyes downcast, let them choose you. Allowing you on their backs is a huge ask of trust, and you must first demonstrate your trust in them. If they eat the berries from your hands, you are free to look at them, but keep your voice and movements gentle, and do *not* touch their horns."

I obeyed, though tearing my gaze away from their beauty felt like tearing away a piece of myself. And after a moment, I was rewarded with a whuff of warm breath across my cheek. The brush of a velvet nose. A ticklish whisker.

Thunder rumbled again, louder this time, but all my attention was focused on the glimpses of this magnificent creature that my downcast eyes could catch. The ripple of muscle under the soft silvery coat. The mirror-bright polished hoof. Then the dark gray muzzle gently lipped the gladberries from my outstretched hands.

My heart leaped with gladness, and I dared to look up.

The stormrider that had chosen me had a dappled

silver coat and liquid black eyes so deep and wild that something inside me stirred in response. Now the storm crackling around me and whipping my hair into a frenzy was exhilarating, intoxicating. Calling me to abandon all the worries that shackled me to the earth, spurring me to embrace freedom, flight.

Ameline spoke into my mind. *Your stormrider's name is Tempest.*

"Tempest." I mouthed the name and found it suited her. She tossed her head in playful assertion, as if to say *Well, of course.*

A quick glance showed a pure white stormrider had chosen Ameline and apparently Griff too since he'd reclaimed his perch upon her shoulder. Bryn was stroking the shoulder of a dark gray, a look of rare unguarded wonder on her face.

I offered my hand to Tempest to sniff again and dared to stroke her silken neck. The muscles arched under my hand.

Then lightning flashed, thunder boomed, and the clouds themselves swooped down to alight upon Tempest's shoulders, forming up into huge, arcing wings three times her length to either side.

Breathtaking. Indeed the air was stolen from my lungs as it whipped around us, tugging my hair loose from its bindings and lashing around my face.

"You may now mount up," shouted Silvyr over the roar of the wind.

But when I stepped closer to Tempest's sleek,

muscular shoulder and the cloud-formed wing set upon it, the shriek and pull of the wind softened, like I'd entered a protective circle. The wind still blew, but gently, affectionately. No longer so fiercely that I could not draw breath or hear nothing else.

Tempest's back was too high for me to mount with any grace, and she seemed too dignified to jump and scramble onto. I hesitated in uncertainty, then almost lost my balance as wind rose in a pillar beneath my boots. *Ah*. That was how it was done.

And then I was astride Tempest's back, my knees tucked beneath the base of her wings, my fingers grasping a tangle of her silken mane.

Lightning flared again, and Tempest's wings moved in slow graceful curves that propelled us upward into the storm. I was awed. I was terrified. But I was mostly filled with a sense of wild abandon as the ground fell away.

We were *flying*. The world darkened as we entered the turbulent chaos of the water-laden clouds. Lightning flashed and thunder boomed all around us. Yet I felt safe on Tempest's back, cocooned in her magic. The rest of the stormriders and those they'd generously deigned to carry flew with us, and far below, the ground sped past at an astonishing pace.

I released my grip on Tempest's mane and reached out my hands in wonder, in exploration. Beyond the protective bubble, the wind thrashed savagely at my fingertips.

I hadn't come to the war front expecting to find joy, but in that moment, elation filled my heart to bursting. I shoved away the cares and concerns wearing on my soul and reveled in the intense feral beauty of the present.

I picked out each of my friends amid the herd of stormriders and saw my elation reflected on their faces. We grinned fiercely at each other, and did not get a single bug in our teeth.

Magic indeed.

Then we came upon the purpose of our flight, and the joy I clutched tore through my fingers like the thrashing wind.

Strange how you can hear something described over and over again in a hundred different ways and yet still fail to grasp the reality until you witness it firsthand.

Stretching below, framed by Tempest's dark gray wing and silver side, was mile upon mile of black roiling darkness.

The Malus was like fog, if fog were black and alive with menace. If fog could rip the life force from any and all living things within its reach (except the hollows who'd given up much to be able to stand in its path). If fog could possess the essence of a creature and use their bodies as puppets for its own ends. If fog could tear down buildings, blind you with its darkness, and flood your mind with fear so great it drove brave men insane. If fog had its own crude intelligence. Insatiable, unstoppable, and intent on devouring the world.

Black menacing fog that seemed to go on forever.

Far, far below along one edge of it, I could see tiny specks that might have been fellow armsmen blazing a stretch of earth. So small, so insubstantial in comparison.

I blinked and looked with my second sight. The blackness was replaced by life force so bright it was like gazing into the sun.

I'd thought the life force in the cache that housed the accumulated life energy of every walker hollow on this planet had been immense. Had imagined being able to change the world with that much power.

The Malus's life force was inconceivable. Diminishing the cache in contrast to that of a puddle compared to the ocean.

How in the world could I ever hope to stop this thing?

It would be like a bug attempting to stop a charging stoneboar. It ended very poorly for the bug, and the stoneboar didn't even notice.

And if I failed, all beauty, all life would be drained from the world.

A vise clamped around my chest, imagining a future where the wonder of the stormriders had been forever extinguished. I let my second sight drop away, preferring to look at the unending darkness rather than the brilliance of the Malus's life force.

That brilliance had been formed by death and horror and sorrow in quantities so great it was unfathomable.

From our vantage high above the monster's grasp, its central core was clearly evident. A yawning hole of darkness so black it seemed to suck the light out of the world around it.

The Malus did not physiologically possess a heart or brain as we understood them, but it had been deduced that this central core was similarly critical to its survival, and its outer darkness more like human limbs in that it could survive their loss. If you shut the Malus's core on one side of a magic gateway and some of the outer, lesser darkness on the other, the "limb" would mindlessly return to the core or else slowly dissipate if there wasn't enough to last the journey. The only true constraint to our enemy's power was distance —and the time and energy it expended to cross it. Meanwhile, the central core of the Malus would go on wreaking destruction.

A courageous expedition of hollows had tried opening a void gate right in the middle of that core, but the intangible darkness merely parted around it, avoiding it neatly and effortlessly. You could no more force the Malus into the void than you could trap fog with a sieve.

That wasn't all they'd tried. I'd read the full history of their attempts at the academy.

For 150 years, thousands of powerful, intelligent,

and determined individuals had thrown themselves against the Malus's might.

Every one of them had ultimately failed.

Could I truly expect to be any different?

The small flame of hope that I'd been carrying with me since that morning in the cache—the flame of hope that had been sparked into being by the prophecy, my wildcard gift, and Theus and Lirielle's conviction that I was the "firstborn human witch" prophesied to defeat the Malus—was in danger of being smothered by the formidable sight below.

So when Tempest and the other stormriders turned back toward the base, I felt only relief.

CHAPTER FOUR

The return journey was a little less wondrous than the ride out. This time I noticed the terrain below. Endless miles of barren, devastated land and vacant ruins the Malus had left in its wake. And I knew that what we flew over was only a fraction of it.

We were a subdued lot that planted our feet back on the dirt and thanked the stormriders for the honor they'd done us. In spite of that, feeding Tempest extra gladberries coaxed a smile to my lips, and not even the Malus could steal my gratitude at having experienced that incredible flight.

Silvyr eyed us with concern, as if wondering whether he'd be blamed for our morose state.

"Don't look so glum," he said. "Old big black blobby isn't so bad once you get used to him."

No one looked convinced.

"Plus if you don't cheer up, I'll whistle again."

We obediently pasted smiles on our faces, but Silvyr's irreverence had in fact made me feel a little better.

We had a few hours to unpack, eat, and settle in before we would receive our new unit assignments. Silvyr directed us toward the sleeping quarters and told us we were free to choose our own arrangements. After six months of sharing a room with Ameline and Bryn, and years before that sharing a bed with Mila, I couldn't imagine sleeping alone. So Ameline, Bryn, and I chose to bunk together in one of the larger shared rooms while Theus and Lirielle took single units nearby.

There was no blood-lock on our bedroom like there had been in Millicent. Now that Ellbereth had stopped trying to kill me, I was hopeful we wouldn't need one, but who knew what the future held? I'd yet to learn how the other armsmen here felt about my reaper magic.

That was another reason not to sleep alone.

Such thoughts reminded me uneasily of the bargain I'd struck to protect Theus. The debt I'd yet to repay.

In many ways we'd exchanged one lethal threat for another. Binding Ellbereth's life to mine had stopped her and her minions from killing me at the academy. But now Theus and I harbored a deadly secret.

One that had been discovered by Lord Perridor before we'd even finished carrying it out.

When he'd caught us in the Cache of the Last Stand, I'd pushed in front of Theus to take the heat. Because in that cache, *I* held the power. The power to drain the life force from any member of walkerkind, hollow or not.

Almost as easily as the Malus could.

Lord Perridor, a member of the ruling walker council, had quickly agreed to keep our deadly secret to himself. A little *too* quickly. He'd even volunteered to actively conceal Theus's involvement from the rest of the council in return for just one "small" favor.

The deal had corrupt written all over it.

I'd agreed anyway.

And it was that favor that hung over my head, waiting for Lord Perridor to call it in.

Unaware of the dark turn my thoughts had taken, Ameline pushed through the lockless door and flopped onto the nearest bed. Her golden hair was snarled and tangled, her hands stained with gladberry juice, and her eyes alight in dreamy remembrance of the stormriders.

"That was *incredible*." Her nose wrinkled. "Flying with the stormriders I mean, not the horrible Malus. Even Griff enjoyed it. Did you know the walkers brought the gladberry plant with them just for the stormriders? And Windswept promised if we destroyed the Malus, they would take us on another flight to celebrate."

Despite my own state of mind, I smiled. Ameline's

28

gentle strength was inspiring to me, and somehow she'd attained it without losing any of her warmth and kindness. She was a daily reminder of all that was worth saving in this world.

Bryn smiled too. Her short black hair had fallen back into its straight lines without effort, and she claimed the next bed and shot me a knowing look. "Sure, tell Windswept to pencil it in next week then. I'm sure it won't take us long now that the prophesied one is here."

I strode to the remaining bed and threw a pillow at her.

She incinerated it before it made contact.

Ameline volunteered to find a replacement.

Beyond the pillow incident, unpacking didn't take long. We laid our paltry possessions in the plain trunks provided, and Griff claimed a spot on the windowsill for his own roost. Then we took turns trying out the walker-style bathroom facilities and changing into our new uniforms (except for the golden body armor) since that was what everyone else seemed to wear around the base.

I offered to use the shower last since I was known to take the longest. By then, Bryn's stomach was grumbling so loudly that I ushered them out the door, promising to meet them at the mess hall when I was done.

My own stomach was still unsettled by the formidable sight of the Malus and its impossible wealth of life force. So when I'd finally finished combing the wind-made knots and snarls from my wet hair, I didn't rush straight to the eatery.

Theus found me standing on the edge of the base, staring out at the horizon. But I wasn't looking at the barren ground this time.

The sky had never seemed so wide hemmed in by the towering trees at the academy nor in the remains of Los Angeles where I'd grown up. It stretched on and on, unobstructed by anything, and I was imagining what the night sky might look like. An endless vista of distant stars.

Sometimes it was comforting to gain a sense of your own unimportance in the greater scheme of things. Except I was no longer sure I could claim that comfort. Not when I sort of believed I was the first-born prophesied to defeat the Malus.

I flashed a welcoming smile at Theus, involuntarily noticing the beauty of his clear-cut features and the smattering of freckles that decorated them. How the closeness of his athletic form just several inches taller than mine made his lips so easily reachable. Or how his deep green eyes had grown warmer and more alluring over the past months.

I turned back to the sky. The sky was a whole lot less complicated than the man beside me.

I'd accepted Theus as a friend even before I'd accepted the walkers were not my enemy. And now that the wall I'd held up between myself and his kind had crumpled since that fateful day in the cache where he'd risked everything for me, it was impossible to deny my feelings.

I cared about him. I trusted him. Wanted only good for him.

More than that, *I wanted him.*

My heart fluttered at his nearness. Like it had never gotten the memo that I didn't have the luxury of being a teenager.

It was a mess of complications I hadn't managed to unravel.

Theus joined me in staring at the horizon, but his attention was on me just as mine was on him.

"I saw your expression when we got back from seeing the Malus," he said. "Being the prophesied one doesn't mean it's all on your shoulders, you know. I won't leave you to face this alone."

"I know," I said.

That truth was both a relief and a burden.

Theus would stick by my side until the end. But that end was exactly what made this so complicated.

I remembered the haunted expression on his face when he'd recounted finding my unmoving body at the bottom of the lake.

How much worse would it have been if we were lovers?

Yet I couldn't help remember too his fingers brushing my cheek as he removed a tangle of wet hair from my face. The light in his eyes as we'd joked around in the forest. The amusement that had broken through his reserve when I'd been practicing my magic on snails. His shock when I'd told him he was worth protecting.

Was it better to grab whatever time we were given? Or wait and see first if we would survive long enough to have a future?

The choice was mine. Theus was too reserved, too self-contained, perhaps too damaged to make the first move. And for as long as I'd known him, he had only ever acted in my best interests, so he was probably too selfless as well.

If I wanted anything to happen, I would have to be the one to initiate it.

I could do that.

But *should* I do that?

Theus was like a deep, deep well. Strong, unstinting, deceptively tranquil, and difficult to explore the depths of.

Yet in my quiet moments, I had sometimes imagined what it might be like to dive down and lead him up to the surface, to the sunlight, the warmth. To reach past the years of hurt, past the dark and rigid scars on his soul, not to ignore them, belittle them, trivialize them, but to show him that those scars made him strong, desirable, beautiful.

But my life as a firstborn had never been about meeting my own desires. My future as the prophesied one even less so.

And I was deeply afraid I would wound Theus further. Break him even. Because if I was right and he felt the same, where would it end?

I knew what I was here to do. And since any chance I had of defeating the Malus would surely require me to draw on massive amounts of life force that no human was ever designed to bear, it seemed almost inevitable that I would either die or die trying.

Perhaps I was frowning at my tangle of thoughts because Theus broke the silence.

"Despite six months at the academy, you never quite caught the hang of true teamwork."

His tone was one of gentle teasing, and I felt my lips tug up in response.

"Oh?"

"You're supposed to share the burden, the responsibility. Not just delegate the actual to-do list."

I snorted at the idea of my to-do list. One, eat lunch. Two, defeat the unstoppable Malus.

"Oh really?" I returned. "And when did you get so good at it? You seem to hold the weight of the world on your shoulders." Never mind he'd spent his whole life being told he was weak.

He smiled in acknowledgment at the accuracy of my observation. "Then we both do. Let us at least hold it together."

My heart clenched at this simple offer. Like everything else Theus had offered me, it was pure, untainted by self-interest, freely given.

I wanted so badly to take it. To take his hand and everything else he might offer too.

But my head advised caution.

I was extricated from this familiar internal wrestle by Silvyr jogging up to us.

"Wildcard Nova, Lord General Zaltarre wants to see you. I'm to escort you to command headquarters immediately."

CHAPTER FIVE

My stomach knotted with nervous tension as I followed Silvyr through a series of gateways to the base that housed the command post.

Lord General Zaltarre, commander of the entire walker-human army of hollow forces, possessed the power to destroy any shred of hope I had of overcoming the Malus. He could force me to go up against the unstoppable devouring force with my hands figuratively tied behind my back.

Or he could arm me with a toilet brush and keep me from seeing any action at all.

My wildcard gift had engendered extreme reactions in walkerkind. Eerily similar to the Malus's life-force-ripping magic, many had wanted to kill me outright. Others believed I was the one who would finally defeat their hated enemy.

Singling me out meant the lord general's feelings

must land on one side or the other, and I was as nervous my first time facing down a groundbeast to learn which.

Silvyr offered no clues. For all his colorful guidance and lively, animated manner, he gave very little of himself away. I hadn't even figured out how *he* felt about me, let alone the unseen lord general. He led me to a building as nondescript as the rest of them and ushered me to the door.

I licked dry lips and pushed it open.

Lord General Zaltarre was standing as I entered, leaning along with several others over a huge table that appeared to be part desk, part magical depiction of the battlefield, showing every unit, base, and mile of terrain spread around the Malus's perimeter. Before I could offer to come back later, the representation of the battlefield retreated into the wood grain of the desk, and his aides swept into adjoining sections of the command building, leaving the two of us alone.

I noted a tray of untouched food cooling (but neatly aligned) on one corner. Then dragged my reluctant gaze up to meet the lord general's.

He cut a trim and fit figure in his military uniform. It was the same as everyone else's except for the pins demarcating his rank. His short, dark, no-nonsense hair was streaked with silver, his square-cut face lined with years and experience. And he possessed a tightly controlled intensity that gave the impression he was extremely busy and yet had all the time necessary to give the current matter his undivided attention.

If he were human, I would've pegged him between a very healthy fifty or sixty. Lord General Zaltarre was a walker, but he was also a hollow, which meant my estimate might not be far off.

He could have been alive when the world walkers retreated to earth, bringing the devastation of the Malus with them. But if so, he would've been ten years old at most. The more interesting takeaway was that he'd likely spent his entire adult life out here, pitting himself against the Malus on the ever-changing war front.

He ran an appraising eye over me.

Something about him made my spine straighten, and I had to fight the urge to salute. The aura of command seemed to emanate from his every pore. Nor was it an empty authority, bestowed by a title alone. I could already tell from the way those off duty spoke about him with almost reverent respect, from how even the irreverent Silvyr hastened to obey his orders, that this authority was earned.

The lord general's gaze was not condescending, merely measuring.

No, he was not arrogant nor fool enough to dismiss the human portion of his army. Not when he needed every warrior he could get.

"I've heard a lot about you, Armsman Nova," he said, and I learned his voice exuded authority too.

"Those reports vary wildly depending on the source. So tell me, what are you? A victim or a troublemaker?"

I wasn't sure what answer he was looking for, but I gave him the truth.

"Neither, sir. I'm here to fight the Malus and no one else." I paused, then felt compelled to add, "Provided I have a choice in the matter."

Something that might have been provisional approval gleamed in his eyes.

"Good. Then let us see what your wildcard power can do."

He signaled for me to take a seat and sat down himself on the other side of the desk in the unyielding, poised-for-action way of someone unused to sitting.

Was the gesture intended for my comfort? It was clearly not for his.

The tray of food remained untouched.

"Armsman Silvyr should have told you that new arrivals usually shadow an experienced unit to learn the ropes before forming their own."

The lord general said this like Silvyr could have just as easily taken us mud sliding down the barren hills rather than given us the intended induction.

Feeling the strange need to defend our jaunty tour guide, I said, "He did, sir."

Lord General Zaltarre smiled briefly. "Very good. In any case, given your unique strategic value, I've decided to form up a special unit around you to learn and utilize your capabilities as soon as possible."

Oh.

Good. That was good, right?

He saw me as an asset rather than an abomination. And he wasn't going to waste time. Which probably meant I'd been right not to give in to my desires with Theus. The sooner started, the sooner done.

You mean dead? Gus interjected. *There is little glory in it. I'd advise avoiding it if you can.*

I contained an eye roll at what my millennia old sword who had probably seen more battles than I had days considered "helpful" advice.

I really must get out of the habit of carrying him with me everywhere I went.

Zaltarre's gaze was still on me, monitoring my reaction. And it belatedly occurred to me that it might not be out of mere courtesy that he was sharing these details with me.

"I don't like to break up units," he continued. "Familiarity and shared experience gives a team an edge that cannot be manufactured any other way. But the chaos of life never fits so neatly into unchanging twelves. Injuries, deaths, personnel clashes, promotions, parental leave, transfer requests and more mean that necessarily there are always some fighters waiting to be reassigned. So your new unit will be assembled from people who, for whatever reason, were among those informally known as the oddments."

His tone acquired an edge of steel.

"Those reasons are *none* of your concern unless the individuals care to share them with you, but they are each competent armsmen. And their range of skill sets and experiences will be an asset that will ensure your unit is ready for action faster than if I left you among only your own year's intake. There is one exception who requested a transfer from the Raptor unit to yours. I believe you grew up with Armsman Fletcher?"

My heart quickened. Fletcher, the boy next door and my dear childhood friend. He'd left a gaping hole in my life when he'd stepped through the runegate to honor the Firstborn Agreement two years before I had. I'd seen him twice since then, and he was so changed I wasn't sure that gaping hole would ever be filled. But the second of those times, Fletcher had made me promise I would request to join his unit.

I'd planned to honor that promise, but now it seemed I wouldn't need to.

"It was good to meet you, Armsman Nova. I trust you'll give me no reason to regret the resources I'm investing in you."

He paused long enough to make my insides squirm.

"Silvyr will take you to meet your new team now. Your unit commander has your orders."

I recognized my dismissal and stood. "Yes, sir. Thank you, sir."

"Oh, and Nova?"

I paused. "Yes?"

"I've designated your team the Reaper unit."

I hid a wince.

All the other units I'd heard of were named after powerful creatures—the Raptors, Fleetfoxes, Embercats, Nightwraiths, and so on. I wasn't keen on breaking that convention to instead name our unit after me and my highly controversial magic.

"Um, as you say, Lord General."

Was that amusement crinkling his eyes? I fled his command room.

CHAPTER SIX

Silvyr grinned at me when I hurried outside.

"Intimidating, isn't he? But he's an excellent general. And if you need any further proof of that, then allow me to be the bearer of extremely good news…" He paused long enough to make me fantasize about wringing his neck. "Your first new team member is none other than myself!"

He made a sweeping gesture up and down the length of his body as if offering himself as a prize.

I raised a brow, not entirely certain if he was messing with me and hoping he'd elaborate.

He eyed me, raised his chin a smidge at my underwhelming response, and went on with his sales pitch.

"You might be wondering how your unit could be so lucky as to be gifted with my abundant wit and charm, and you may go on and continue wondering, for I'm also a man of great mystery and intrigue."

I hoped my unbidden smirk wouldn't encourage him too much. But he must have caught it because he puffed up his chest in parody and made some dramatic walker flourish. "Let me escort you to meet the rest of your unit, my most esteemed and precious wildcard."

I trailed after him, part apprehension, part curiosity. Reminded again that I did not tend to make friends easily. Not that I *needed* to be friends with my unit, I supposed, but... well, it would sure make things easier.

We returned to our base through a succession of short-distance gateways and walked to one of the smaller shared areas where ten uniformed figures stood waiting.

Silvyr gestured at the four that were smiling. "These younglings from the thirty-seventh I understand you already know and like."

Indeed. Zaltarre had done his homework, or at least read whatever reports he received from the academy. Everyone was here. Ameline, Bryn, Theus, and Lirielle.

I felt a swell of gladness. Then wondered if my older wiser self might've wished them far from me where they might be safer.

Silvyr moved on to an older walker woman I didn't recognize. "So let me first introduce you to our formidable leader. Her tongue is as sharp as her sword, her skill on the battlefield as shiny as her boots, she's the illustrious and demanding and most commanding, Unit Commander Valesk of the seventeenth and designated head of our ragtag, ahem, glorious unit."

She scowled at Silvyr and nodded curtly at me. Not looking happy at... What? Silvyr's silly introduction? Her new assignment? The world in general?

Unit Commander Valesk was meticulously turned out, her boots, belt, and body armor polished, her uniform immaculate, and her black hair braided with such precision that I had the fleeting impression she'd marshaled the strands into position like a troop of soldiers and ordered them to stand their ground, or else. She too stood ramrod straight as if setting a good example.

Being part of the seventeenth intake meant she must be thirty-seven or thirty-eight years old, depending on the month of her birth, and that she'd been on the war front for twenty years. I wondered what had happened to her original unit to leave her without one, but the lord general's warning was fresh in my mind, so I did not ask.

Unsure what else to do, since saluting was not actually part of walker military culture, I nodded back.

Silvyr moved on to another face I knew. One so familiar and yet foreign at the same time. My much-changed childhood friend.

"Armsman Fletcher from the thirty-fifth, whom I understand you're also acquainted with and so needs no introduction."

Zaltarre had said Fletcher left his own unit to transfer to this one, but there was little but stiffness in his face now.

As always, the sight of him flooded me with mixed feelings. The first leap of joyous recognition before my brain finished registering all the differences, and then the loss.

I wanted to grieve, for in some ways the boy I knew was no more than a ghost, and yet how could you grieve for someone who was standing in front of you?

I stepped forward, hesitated, then hugged him anyway. I hadn't the last time I'd seen him, and I'd regretted it.

He went rigid, and for a horrible moment I wondered if I'd misjudged, but then he relaxed, hugged me back, and whispered, "I'm glad you're here." And his face was a little less hard when I stepped back.

Silvyr was watching our exchange with interest, but as soon as my attention returned to him, he moved on to the next members of my new unit.

I suspected his mind was far sharper than his airy manner let on.

"These two muscle-bound hunks are Armsmen Orlandrus and Dax of my own prestigious intake, the thirty-first. They're as inseparable as lovers; in fact, rumor has it they are indeed lovers"—this did not elicit so much as a twitch of an eyebrow from either of the men—"and they're known collectively as the Grunts. They're also the proud defending champions of Blob Blast, and between them have almost as much intelligence as anyone else."

By the end of this colorful introduction, I was smiling, which was at least preferable to revealing my surprise. Because their close friendship—or love—had crossed the divide between the species. Orlandrus was a walker and Dax a human.

The past three months of trust building and team exercises at the academy had improved walker-human relations among my own year's intake, but there were still invisible lines separating one from the other in most instances. I was beginning to grasp that here on the war front, those lines had been erased.

I nodded at them as well, and Orlandrus flashed white teeth. "What, don't we get hugs too?"

I felt my cheeks heat. I was used to coldness, condescension, and even hatred from walkerkind, but friendly flirting with an admittedly attractive stranger was new to me.

I didn't want to be known as some blushing flower though, so I scrambled for something suitably cocky to say.

"Maybe after we're done killing the Malus."

It took a beat too long, but it was better than standing there looking like I'd rubbed gladberry juice on my face.

Orlandrus and Dax grinned appreciatively.

"Aiming high," Dax said. "I like that. You should play Blob Blast with us sometime."

He had a light lilting accent I couldn't place, but then there were very few accents I *could* place. I liked it in any case.

Silvyr cleared his throat. He'd waited until I'd already dug myself out of the awkward situation, and I pondered again just how keenly he was observing me. Was he reporting to someone? Say, the lord general, for example? Or Ellbereth's mother, Lady Neryndrith?

Or perhaps having a lethal secret that I had to keep was making me paranoid.

The next team member was so badly scarred that if it wasn't for his beautiful bright copper eyes and his utter stillness, it would've been difficult to tell if he was walker or human. The hair that grew between the crisscrosses of scars on his scalp was peppered with gray, and his right hand was not flesh but rather animated metal like the squeakers. I wondered how far that metal continued up past his shirtsleeve.

"This lethal gentleman is Armsman Xanther of the thirteenth," Silvyr announced. "Contrary to popular belief, his tongue is still made of flesh and he can in fact speak. He merely chooses not to. I'm chagrined to admit he's probably more mysterious than me. But while we might be left to wonder at his unshared thoughts, there are no questions whatsoever about his fighting prowess on the battlefield."

I gave Xanther the same nod as I'd given everyone

else. I couldn't tell if his chin dipped a fraction in response or if I was being optimistic, but his bright copper gaze punched through me before looking away.

Silvyr stepped up to the twelfth and final member of my new team. A white-haired woman who looked around the same age as Lord General Zaltarre and almost as fit.

"Finally but most fabulously, our aged and esteemed Armsman Helena of the third, who has survived twice as many years on this war front as you have lived and saved more armsmen than I can count with her healing gift."

"Enough years and lives that I shouldn't have to put up with your nonsense, Silvyr," she said in a heavy accent. But the light in her eyes seemed at least as amused as unimpressed. She reached out a hand and shook mine firmly. "Pleased to meet you, Wildcard Nova."

She did not look at me with the same hopeful calculation that the lord general had. How many times had she seen wildcards and other promising new prospects come and go and amount to nothing?

Unit Commander Valesk cut in. "Now that the introductions are *finally* completed, we have a mission to carry out."

Everyone else must have already been briefed on our unit's unusual formation and my wildcard gift because Valesk didn't say anything more about it. I belatedly realized that all my new team members were wearing their shield nets, weapons, body armor, and squeakers. Ameline handed me mine, except Gus who I already had with me, and I geared up. My personal squeaker was a cute squirrel-like creature with turquoise gemstones for eyes and a long tail it wrapped around my ear.

Valesk had us newbies run through the use of our shield nets several more times. As we dove to the dirt, the squeaker quietly relayed several amused snorts from our more experienced teammates, along with Valesk's orders, which I could have heard perfectly well without the little squirrel's assistance.

Its mimicry was, as Silvyr had said, near perfect except for a tinny undertone, and if there was any delay between Valesk speaking and my squeaker relaying the words to me, it was undetectable to my ears.

I made a mental note to keep my own mouth shut. I was definitely going to have to change my habit of muttering to Gus aloud.

"That will do," Valesk said. "Form up for a final inspection."

She made a show of scanning over each of us and our equipment, but she stopped in front of me.

"Armsman Nova, let me be clear. The Reaper unit might have been created for and even named after your unique gift. But I am in charge and you *will* obey my orders. You might be used to special status"—did she mean loathed by almost everyone at the academy?

—"but there's no room for special treatment when we're within the enemy's grasp. You will do what I say when I say because that will give us the highest chance of protecting your ass and getting us all back to this base alive."

Her hard gaze shifted suddenly to my left. "Isn't that right, Fletcher?"

Confused, I glanced at my old friend, who flinched and looked like he wanted to crawl inside himself and disappear. But he only said, "Yes, sir."

The hard gaze landed back on me. "Are we clear?"

"Yes, sir. Understood."

"Good. Let's move."

CHAPTER SEVEN

Contrary to Cricklewood's prediction, none of us wet ourselves when we faced the Malus for the first time. Perhaps that was in part thanks to Silvyr's special tour that had allowed us to come to terms with its immensity from a safer distance.

The acrid stench of scorched earth and trees turned to charcoal permeated the air. But that was a result of our own side's efforts rather than the enemy's.

Here on the outer edges, the Malus was like a faint black haze. Difficult to see over the charred landscape. Impossible to see at night without my second sight. In some places the black haze mingled with the occasional still-smoking tree stump.

But the darkness grew denser the deeper you ventured inward. Turning into a blackness so complete it smothered all light and rendered you sightless.

An unwanted flash of insight left me wondering

just how many members of this army slept with some form of illumination. The Malus's creeping, lethal advance could leave even the bravest soul afraid of the dark.

I checked my weapons, my shield net, my strange new communication device.

Gus huffed. *Can you please stop all this hand-hovering business? You don't need to check I'm still attached every ten seconds. As much as I might wish to, I have not managed to grow legs and do away with your esteemed company.*

"Sorry," I said, so distracted that I forgot my resolve to avoid conversing with him aloud.

"What for?" someone, I think Orlandrus, asked.

"Don't mind, Nova," Bryn said. "She's just talking to her sword. Even weirder is she claims it talks back."

A few people chuckled.

I sighed.

Standing on the perimeter gave a fresh perspective of the size of our enemy. I knew from the air it was roughly circular, but here on the edge all I could see was darkness that seemed to stretch without end in either direction. From the sky, I'd been unable to grasp its height. Now it reared up and up, blocking out the heavens as it towered menacingly over us like the front of a catastrophic sandstorm.

No wonder watch duty took up so much of the lord general's resources.

My squeaker mimicked a low whistle. "Holy

kraken cakes," Bryn, or the squeaker, whispered in my ear. "That thing makes poor Choppy seem under-sized." Choppy was her giant magical battle-axe. It didn't have sentience like Gus, but she'd named it anyway.

Dax's voice came next. "If you think that's big, you should see my—"

"No personal chatter over the comm lines when we're in sight of the enemy," Valesk growled. "You can save your adolescent innuendo for when you're off duty."

"Sorry, Unit Commander. I was just trying to keep up… morale."

Boyish snickers.

How old were Orlandrus and Dax supposed to be again?

Still, the silly banter brought a touch of normalcy to this alien landscape and the enemy before us.

We weren't expecting trouble. But then how could we have any idea *what* to expect when I was about to try something that had never been done before?

I took a deep breath. "Ready to make the first attempt, Unit Commander."

"Good. The rest of you, form up around her in case of attack. Weapons and shield nets ready."

Despite the immature banter, Orlandrus and Dax moved into position as swiftly and competently as the silent and scarred Xanther.

I entrusted my physical safety to my new unit's

care, stole one last glance at each of my friends—Ameline, Bryn, Theus, Lirielle, and Fletcher—then turned my focus solely on my second sight. I could see the glow of life force as an overlay to my natural vision, but I could see more clearly if I shut my eyes. So that's what I did.

As my second sight adjusted to the incredibly bright glare of the Malus, I realized there was something else I hadn't grasped from our overhead flight. Its glowing life force was unlike any I'd seen before.

Flying high above on Tempest's back with my eyes still open, I'd noticed it had a sort of mottled quality, but I'd assumed it had to do with the enemy's movement. I'd assumed wrong.

Other creatures' life forces appeared to me as a solid golden light that followed the shape of their physical form and grew softer on the edges. Different beings had different strengths, with weaker life forms showing as dimmer and more transparent, and solid obstacles or distance decreased the clarity of what I could see. But the light of their life force, however bright, was always uniform, even, consistent.

The Malus broke this rule.

First I saw only that it was thinner in some patches and more opaque in others. But as I stared, I realized it was stranger than that.

Other life forces existed within the Malus's. As if it took the devouring darkness time to assimilate the stolen energy into itself.

The *other* beings were fuzzier and less well-defined than a normal living creature's, and many were no more than a slightly brighter blob, but others were identifiable. A manticore there, some sort of giant hawk over there, a faded but still apparent form of a dragon.

Fascinating.

But irrelevant as far as I could tell. It certainly didn't impact what I'd come here to attempt. And the longer I stood here dallying, the longer I was leaving my teammates in danger.

Time to get to work.

My magic brushed the edge of the Malus's life force. I'd developed subtlety over the past couple of months, finding I could lessen my donor's resistance if I could keep my touch light, the draw smooth. At least until I took their life force down to dangerous levels. Then the instinctive resistance kicked in no matter how delicate my connection.

Now my touch was the lightest I could make it, lighter than a gentle caress, no more than the faint brush of magical fingertips.

Nothing happened.

I'm not sure what I expected. Instant death? Recognition? But I felt nothing except the vibrant hum of energy beneath my touch.

The fact I could feel it at all was positive. With other living beings, I was unable to interact with their life force unless I first drew blood, breaching the protection their body offered. But without a tangible physical form, the Malus was accessible to my magic like the sundered life force of the walker hollows inside the cache. There for the taking.

Maybe.

Cautiously I pressed a little harder, a little deeper. No reaction. Gently, ever so gently, I gave the Malus's life force a slight tug.

That was when the Malus yanked back.

CHAPTER EIGHT

The force of the Malus's pull was like being attached to a landslide, beginning slowly but building to greater and greater strength and speed. Unstoppable.

I magically planted my feet and wrenched back with all my strength. But even as I did, my mind was racing on ahead to the inevitable end.

Panic bloomed in my chest and spread like an invasive weed.

I was utterly outmatched.

And I was terrifyingly certain the Malus was stealing my life force. Something I'd thought impossible.

Which meant being a human hollow didn't protect me from the Malus's life-ripping magic. Not entirely like it did for the rest of my unit.

Which meant my oh-so-special wildcard gift must

circumvent the protections of having my life force anchored elsewhere—theoretically far from the Malus's grasp. Must have formed a connection between my life energy and the one I was trying to siphon from. In effect, my oh-so-special wildcard gift offered me up before the Devourer on a stupid golden platter.

Oh sure, the enemy could not just reach out and pluck it from me like it could with other living things. But as soon as I latched onto *its* life force, the Malus could latch onto mine.

Which meant I was going to die.

Even resisting, wrenching, and twisting as hard as I could, the Malus's pull on my life force, my essence, was speeding up.

I could feel myself weakening. Could feel the life *literally* draining out of me.

Oh hells. I wasn't freaking ready to die.

But this was a contest of brute force I couldn't possibly win.

Unless…

With desperate panicked thoughts of tricking a dog into loosening their grip in a game of tug-of-war, I stopped resisting.

My life force hurtled forward into the golden light of the Malus. And I had just enough time to think, *Well, that backfired.*

Then everything went black.

Except my consciousness remained.

Was this dying then? Or was I still in the process of dying and the Malus had taken so much that I'd lost my ability to see?

But the pull, the movement, the momentum had stopped too.

Perhaps it had stolen my senses and I would be left to wander in the dark nothingness until my golden life energy lost all form and fully assimilated into the Malus—

"Nova."

My ears still worked. And Theus sounded so near, so intimate. Like his face was only inches from mine. I almost fancied I could feel the stir of his breath.

Perhaps this was death after all and I was allowed to dream of everything that had been wrenched from me.

"Nova." It was Theus's voice again, but this time he shook me.

Wait. What?

There was a jolt of disorientation as my under-standing snapped back.

I opened my eyes. My *actual* eyes. My second sight was still as dark as the grave. But my natural eyes worked fine.

Theus was leaning over me. His face really was only inches from mine. And just a fraction farther away were Ameline and Bryn's faces too.

The terror in their expressions snatched the air from my lungs. And not in a good way. I knew first-hand of their strength and spirit and courage, and that terror was for losing me.

Theus whooshed out an unsteady breath and released me to rake his fingers through his hair.

Almost as jarringly as when it had failed, my second sight surged back.

Ameline clutched my hand so hard it hurt. "Oh, thank heavens. I thought…"

Bryn shook her head, her usual bravado quickly resurfacing. "Hairy hellish hobgoblins, we didn't go to all that effort of saving your ass at the academy only for you to die in the first five minutes after graduating."

I sat up shakily. So, so weak, and yet somehow alive and wanting to reassure my friends of that fact.

"What?" I croaked. "That wasn't the roaring success you were hoping for?"

No one had time to even pretend to laugh, because Ameline grabbed for her bow and announced, "Griff says there are Taken coming our way fast."

Her loyal companion had insisted on flying high above the Malus's grasp to provide us intel from the air.

From my semi-upright position, I saw a shadow stalker, an eleven-headed hydra, and a handful of other vicious creatures emerge from the cloaking black fog of the Malus.

Unit Commander Valesk issued calm but terse orders. "Theus, get Nova out of here now. Everyone else, protect each other's backs, especially the newbies', and let's destroy a few of the enemy's toys."

CHAPTER NINE

Theus opened a gateway beneath us, only daring to venture a few hundred yards for the first stage of our retreat. I could see the Taken—creatures whose life force had been seized by the Malus and were now mere puppets at its disposal—charging at my teammates before Theus opened the second gateway.

"Dibs on the hydra," Orlandrus and Dax said in unison.

Bryn huffed a laugh and readied a fireball. "Well I've still got a score to settle with shadow stalkers. I've been wondering for some time whether their eyes are as fireproof as the rest of them."

Lirielle drew her twin swords—even though she had powerful magic she could've called upon instead.

There was something about holding those blades that drew her mind back from the faraway places it usually wandered and focused her in the present. It made her seem sort of normal, which was disconcerting on Lirielle.

"I did miss sword practice this morning," she remarked.

Ameline stood straight-backed and poised, despite not having any magic to protect her besides that of her bow. Fletcher stepped up beside her, broadsword raised.

Then Theus and I retreated through a second gateway, and I had only the squeaker in my ear to gauge the well-being of those we'd left behind.

The squeaker relayed several grunts, but I couldn't tell who'd made them nor hear any sounds from the fight itself.

At least there hadn't been any screams.

"Ha!" Dax said. "Take that you big scaly bastard."

"Silvyr, behind you," Orlandrus warned.

Silvyr cursed.

Xanther of course remained silent.

"Eww, who knew barbecued shadow stalker insides smelled so bad?" That was Bryn.

"Griff says we have giant bat-spiders incoming."

"Fletcher," Valesk said, "shield us from above. Make it difficult for them."

There was a minute of silence, and my heart felt like it was beating at twice its normal rate. Waiting. I hated waiting.

"Damn, that's gross," Silvyr said. "I'll be washing bat guts out my hair for days."

I exhaled in relief. He wouldn't be complaining about bat guts if someone was seriously hurt.

"You ought to be more concerned about possible poisoning than washing your hair," Helena chided. "Let me see if any of that blood's yours."

Then Valesk spoke again. "Theus, where are you? What's your status?"

"Safe. Just a few miles out."

"Good. Meet us back at the base for debriefing. I want to understand exactly what the hell happened today."

The Reaper unit gathered around one of the smaller common areas in various states of composure, grubbiness, and fatigue. But everyone was whole and accounted for, so I was tiredly trying to convince myself that my first encounter had been something *other* than an abject failure. Which was hard to do when Valesk, who still looked immaculate, was frowning at me.

"What happened? All Helena could tell me was that your life force was draining fast and there was nothing she could do."

I valiantly resisted the urge to frown back. "That's accurate." I explained what I'd done, what I'd experienced, and my theory that my own magic had circumvented the protection being a hollow gave me.

"Well, crap," Silvyr put in helpfully.

He'd either exaggerated the amount of bat guts or had a talent for magical hair washing.

"Then what saved you?" Valesk demanded.

I'd been wracking my brain, trying to figure out the same thing. Could it have been my bond with Ellbereth? I didn't understand how that would work or why my second sight had shut down and then sprung back after… How long had it been? Less than a minute? But I could think of no other explanation.

The problem was I couldn't share even that feeble speculation. As guilty as I felt about failing to disclose potentially vital information to the unit assigned to work with and protect me, I'd known Valesk and the others for less than a day. I didn't trust them yet with a secret that could get Theus executed and me imprisoned or executed along with him. So all I said was, "I don't know."

Theus surprised me by volunteering, "I think I might have had something to do with it, sir. When I made contact with Nova, I felt a surge of power leave me. Except I wasn't intentionally casting anything, and it felt different to anything I've experienced before. Like the whole world compressed for a minute and something clamped down over my magic. But Nova opened her eyes about thirty seconds later."

I stared at Theus. Had his mind gone to the same places mine had about Ellbereth? Was he making this up to try to cover for me? Or was this real?

For the first time since meeting Gus, I wished for the ability to read someone else's thoughts.

Valesk was staring at Theus now too, tapping one finger against her jaw.

"Are you sure it was your own magic casting rather than the Malus snatching the power from you somehow?"

"Quite sure, sir."

"What were you thinking at the time?"

This was key. Magic was funneled and given shape by intention, willpower, and imagination.

Theus's cheeks tinged with a trace of red. "Stop! You can't have her."

That hint of color in his cheeks convinced me more than anything that he wasn't making this up.

It also convinced part of me that I really ought to kiss him. But I tried to focus on the implications of the former.

What did that mean? *Stop.* Stop what? Surely he couldn't have the strength to magically force the Malus to let go of me. Yet the Malus *had* let go of me. Why?

I pondered some more. Theus might've been directing his thoughts at the Malus, but he'd grabbed *me*. What if… I ran over the sequence of events in my mind again. Yes. My second sight had jolted back on as soon as Theus had let go.

"What if he somehow stopped my magic from working?" I asked. "Without my magic, the connection I'd unintentionally forged with the Malus would cease to exist. Plus it would explain the weird glitchy behavior of my second sight."

Valesk nodded. "It's plausible. Theus, try to reproduce what happened. The more accurately you can recapture what you were feeling and thinking and doing, the better."

Poor Theus.

I readied my second sight and focused on Griff, who was preening his feathers on Ameline's shoulders. As the only non-hollow here, he would provide a clear indicator of whether this worked (though I supposed the shrub growing up through the stone paving would do just as well).

Theus stepped in front of me and gripped my shoulders with an expression of intense concentration, his face furrowed in remembered distress.

My stomach heated at his nearness, his touch. Which was ridiculous given the situation.

I belatedly remembered to look at Griff. He'd disappeared from my second sight. I closed my eyes to double check, and like my experience on the battle-field, everything was black.

"Wow. Yes, it worked. I mean, I can't see anything's life force."

Theus let go and once again the light flooded back. I opened my eyes to find Theus staring at his hands.

"You saved me," I pointed out quietly. His green eyes met mine, and for a moment there was wonder in them.

Theus, who'd been unloved, unvalued, told his entire life he was weak and worth less because his magic was meager by walker standards, had saved my life—the *prophesied* firstborn's life—from the most powerful and fearsome enemy in walker history. With his own unique magic no less.

"Try it on me," Silvyr demanded. He conjured five delicate spheres of light and began juggling them.

Theus touched his arm and the spheres vanished.

"Can you do it without contact?" Valesk asked.

Silvyr and Theus repeated the attempt. But this time Silvyr's spheres kept spinning.

Valesk pursed her lips. "A magic dampener. Very rare. And I suppose the requirement to touch the wielder would explain why you never discovered the ability before now. Not much contact in a magic skirmish..." She frowned, the expression more at home on her face than any other. "But you're the first walker I've heard of with that ability in over three hundred years."

Lirielle smiled beatifically. "That's because he's the prophesied one."

Unbidden, the relevant line of the prophecy floated into my mind. Theus had translated it as *Wait for the world walker magic glitch.* It could certainly be interpreted to mean a world walker that could "glitch" other beings' magic.

Pity he couldn't *touch* the Malus. Not that he'd

have any more hope of directly overpowering the vastness of its strength than I did.

Valesk looked no happier than she had at the beginning of the conversation, but at least her focus had turned inward now. "Time will tell, I suppose. In the meanwhile, I'd best report these developments to the lord general. Everyone else get some rest and be ready for the next set of orders."

Rest sounded good. I was exhausted, although no doubt less exhausted than I might've been without Ellbereth's life energy feeding into mine. I dragged myself to our private quarters, Ameline and Bryn sticking close in case I needed propping up.

All I wanted was to unstrap my unused and overly heavy sword, then stand in the shower and let the hot water wash the stiffness from my muscles and the soot out of my hair from my unplanned lie-down on the freshly scorched perimeter. But when I stepped into the shower, the glass was already fogged, and inscribed into the moisture was a note.

The time has come to pay your debt. Come to the walker city and meet me in the Remembrance Garden at midnight tonight.

Cold unease spread through my gut. For two months I'd known this day was coming. I just hadn't known *when*.

Or who, or why, but never mind that.

It had been a damned if you do and damned if you don't situation. If Theus and I hadn't gone to the cache to bind Ellbereth's life force to mine, she would have killed me. But Theus's taking me there meant betraying his people and signing his own death warrant. Walkers didn't do lifelong imprisonment.

So when Lord Perridor had caught us red-handed in the Cache of the Last Stand—a place forbidden for humans to have even heard of and one impossible to get to without the aid of a walker—I'd bargained for Theus's life. And now it was time for me to keep my side of that bargain.

But hell's breath, it was a debt I wished I could wriggle out of. Lord Perridor, proud member of the ruling walker council, had promised to stay silent and cover up Theus's involvement in exchange for my performing "one simple act." Drain an unnamed walker into unconsciousness at a time and place of Lord Perridor's choosing.

Theus hadn't wanted me to agree. Hadn't thought his life was worth that price.

I'd ignored him and bemused Lord Perridor by shaking hands on the deal (a human custom I tended to forget walkers were unfamiliar with).

In truth, I would have agreed to more than that to protect Theus. I suppose I was already falling for him even then. But more than that, he was a friend who'd risked his life for mine, and everything in me was wired to protect those I cared about.

So yes, I'd known this was coming. And it wasn't like Lord Perridor had asked me to *kill* this unknown target. So why was unease eating away at my stomach lining?

I read the note again, committing the details to memory before it faded away.

I had five hours until it was time to leave. I'd better make sure no one would miss me.

CHAPTER TEN

What does one wear on a criminal foray deep in the heart of their former enemy's capital?

I opted for my uniform stripped of its insignia, largely because I didn't have any other options.

My mouth was drier than megalith moth dust as I made my way to meet Theus and Lirielle. Somehow I felt more nervous about what I was on the brink of doing than I had about my first attempt to pit my magic against the Malus. And *that* had almost gotten me killed.

Without Theus, I *would* have been killed, I reminded myself. And if I hadn't made this bargain, as unsavory as it was, Theus wouldn't have survived long enough to be there when I encountered the Malus. So then we'd both be dead. Which meant I needed to stop second-guessing myself. Right?

Sure. That made perfect sense. But my mouth was still as dry as moth dust.

Theus and Lirielle were waiting at the designated spot a short walk outside the base. They were both wearing their uniforms as I was, which as an added bonus blended well with the darkness.

We probably didn't want to be seen tonight. Not that Lirielle's abundance of frost-colored hair was any good for stealth.

Bryn and Ameline had reluctantly agreed to stay behind and cover for our absence. Only because even Bryn had to concede that Theus and Lirielle's firsthand knowledge and walker blood would prove more useful in the walker city.

We greeted each other in hushed tones, and Theus opened a gateway. Even in stealth, we stuck to the rigid rules regarding multiple short-distance gateways until we were more than a thousand miles away. The Malus traveled relatively slowly under normal conditions, but it had the ability to surge across vast distances in seconds if suitably motivated. Doing so consumed a significant amount of its stolen life energy, so it rarely used the ability unless it was starving or sufficiently tempted with huge amounts of fresh "food."

But if it *did* choose to surge when someone had opened a gateway to one of the few yet untouched regions of the world, the results would be catastrophic.

So every walker approached and exited via the

barren lands to ensure no abundance of life force would tempt the Malus to surge. And even then everyone stuck to short distances because a smaller sudden shift in the Malus's location still posed all sorts of risks and problems for the army.

The modest containment and control the lord general's forces had over the Malus was a dangerous and difficult balance between keeping its advancement, destruction, and life intake to a minimum while ensuring it was satiated enough not to surge.

But all that fell from my mind when we stepped through the last gateway.

Like its creators, the walker city was achingly beautiful. More like an elaborate art garden than any city I'd heard or read about.

My first impression was of elegant ivory stairways, soaring arches, and delicate sky bridges intermingling with an abundance of greenery. The splendor of it was lit by soft floating lights that danced in a grand choreography I couldn't quite grasp and accompanied by a serenade of running water. Even the air felt fresher and smelled sweeter here.

Unlike human cities, the walkers had no need to design their settlement around transportation. So while footpaths wound tantalizingly through the various delights, there were no unsightly roads marring the view or imposing harsh lines. Likewise, the dwellings and buildings were haphazardly placed throughout the canyon with no thought of distance or height or access, but somehow blending harmoniously to the magnificence of this place.

Humans in the Before, for all their technology, had been constrained by physics and materials. Magic overrode such limitations.

As I followed Theus and Lirielle down one of the delicate winding walkways, it was clear the walkers had turned their gift of life magic into an art form. Every thriving shrub, tree, vine, and ground cover had been chosen for its color, its flowers, its fragrance, or its fruit. Living trees spread their branches into glorious archways, flowering vines curled up staircases and pillars, offering heady scents to passersby, and rich green shrubs bowed under the weight of plump ripe fruit that grew at a convenient picking height.

It was like another world. Which gave me a sudden glimpse of understanding for the yearning on Theus's face when he spoke of walking between worlds, of wonder and delighted exploration, and the true cost of what they'd lost.

Lirielle and her floating, ethereal loveliness, who always seemed a little out of place in the halls of the academy and the austere bland functionality of the base, blended in seamlessly here. Like she belonged.

Theus looked... uncomfortable. Stupidly gorgeous, but uncomfortable. And I was reminded that for all this city's splendor, he had few happy memories of this place.

Glorifying beauty and power and perfection might

result in... well, beauty and power, but it was far from perfect.

I reached out and squeezed his hand.

Surprise, then warmth and gratitude flitted across his handsome face. His gladness at the simple gesture stirred old fury at walkerkind for what they'd done to him.

But what they'd done to humankind was worse.

Even so, we needed these imperfect beings, dripping with life magic, to keep our broken world from dying. We needed them to help feed and protect those who had survived the invasion. We needed them to aid us in fighting the monstrosity they'd cursed us with.

And if we managed that impossible feat, we needed them to heal our world afterward.

The walkways were quiet, and we came to the Remembrance Garden without incident.

I immediately understood its name. Huge towering statues depicting creatures I didn't recognize, creatures from other worlds presumably, towered over us in silent, frozen vigil. So exquisitely carved that it seemed as if they might shift position or leap into life at any moment.

The effect was haunting and yet alluring too. I could've spent hours studying these huge lifelike figures. But I didn't have the luxury.

Theus looked up at the same looming figure that had snared my gaze: a two-legged creature distantly resembling a minotaur with a crown of vicious curling horns. Its muscular, furry body was mostly concealed in fine garments, and the artist had captured a look of heartbreaking sorrow in its dangerous features.

"This garden has become unpopular as more and more years passed without world walking," Theus murmured. "I assume that's why he chose it."

"Indeed." Lord Perridor stepped down from another walkway, his eyes flicking dismissively over Theus before landing on me.

"I'm pleased to see you're intelligent enough to pay your debts, Wildcard Nova."

Lirielle didn't react to Perridor's presence, continuing to wander around the garden, stroking the statues like they were old friends.

Theus bristled beside me. "If only *you* were brave enough to do your own dirty work rather than resorting to manipulation."

Lord Perridor appeared unruffled by the accusation, his expression something akin to pity.

"Oh my, I've almost forgotten what it was like to be so young and righteously ignorant. Cowardice has nothing to do with it, my boy. Strategy is a far more fruitful course than self-sacrificial bravery." He paused, then smiled in my direction. "Useful as such a quality can be in one's associates."

I suppressed a wince. That answer would not help Theus feel more comfortable about tonight.

"Who do you want her to drain, and why?" my friend demanded.

"Why was never part of our agreement. As for who. Well… he lives over there in the house on the peak. The deed must be done by one o'clock this morning."

Theus grew even more rigid. "That's council member Lord Brackenfort's home."

"Yes," Perridor answered easily. "Here's an image of his likeness to ensure you get the right man."

He handed it to me and strolled back up the sky bridge without another word.

CHAPTER ELEVEN

"I don't like this," Theus growled.

Neither did I, but I was trying not to dwell on it. A large part of me was *glad* I didn't know Lord Perridor's reasons. Ignorance was bliss. Or at least less internal conflict than if I knew the true consequences of my actions. Right?

Right.

What did I care for walker politics? It's not like I was going to kill the man.

Besides, just because Lord Brackenfort was another council member didn't mean it had anything to do with the council itself. Theus had checked the council's agenda before we'd come tonight, and they weren't even due to meet for another two days, by which time Lord Brackenfort should've recovered.

"I didn't like binding myself to Ellbereth either," I

reminded Theus, "but I did it to survive. And I'm doing this for the same reason. Survival. Yours."

His frown deepened, but he didn't keep arguing. I liked that about him.

I stretched my mouth into a smile. "Now, um, any tips on breaking in?"

"House on the peak" turned out to mean house on top of a really steep vertical column of earth and rocks. And since every walker home had alarm systems for unauthorized magic use, the closest Lirielle and Theus could translocate me was to a small outcrop of rock ten yards from the top.

The three of us barely fit standing shoulder to shoulder to shoulder. Which made it an inconvenient location for a heated debate.

"I'm going alone," I reiterated. "If I get into trouble, I'll yell and you two will be close enough to hear me and rush to my aid. If I don't get into trouble, it's best that we keep your involvement to a minimum."

"There's a flaw in your logic," Theus pointed out. "If you fail to find trouble, what need is there for us to keep our involvement to a minimum?"

"Don't make me push you off this rock," I retorted. Mostly to cover for the fact that I didn't have a good counterargument. "I'm the one that made this deal, so I'll see it through. Besides, it's not like you can borrow my reaper magic and do it for me."

"More's the pity," Theus muttered.

"I like how it feels closer to the stars up here," Lirielle put in, staring out at the sky. "Also, it's twenty minutes to one o'clock."

"I'll yell *really* loud," I promised a final time, and heaved myself up the steep rock face.

Adrenaline thrummed through me, sloughing away my fatigue. And in a weird way I was almost looking forward to a "mission" where the goal might actually be achievable for a change.

When stealing onto someone's private property and draining them close to death felt like a welcome change of pace, you had to question your life choices.

Yet when I thought over the path that had led me here, I couldn't find a crossroads where I could've chosen any differently. Not if I wanted to be able to live with myself.

So I'd just have to make this path work.

The climb was merely a fun challenge if I didn't consider the hundred-yard drop below or my purpose for ascending. I scrambled up as quickly as I dared, careful of the loose stone that crumbled beneath my weight and tumbled merrily downward. In just a few minutes, I reached the top and levered myself over the edge.

Stretching out before my nose and stinging hands

was an ethereal garden that still had the power to amaze even after everything else I'd witnessed.

Lord Brackenfort must indeed be fond of the stars, because in the darkness the garden was lit to appear like an extension of the night sky that stretched in grand display all around us. The extensive foliage was left unilluminated to mimic the inky blackness of the sky's canvas, while bright pinpricks of light were distributed in reminiscence of the distant luminous balls of gas that watched over our world.

Unfortunately for me, those pinpricks of light offered very little illumination for someone trying to sneak through the obstacles in Lord Brackenfort's garden. Nor could I use Ellbereth's magic to create my own without alerting him to my presence. So using my fingers and careful steps to find obstacles before I noisily collided with them, I crept slowly through the pretty darkness toward the large starlit structure I assumed was Lord Brackenfort's home.

As I drew closer, I saw that the entire front of the house and most of the sloped ceiling was made of glass. Just as well I hadn't made that light. But how did you creep up on a see-through house?

I skirted around to the right where I thought the outer cladding of the home changed to something less transparent. With luck I wouldn't accidentally and abruptly find the other edge of the steep rock column in the dark.

Lirielle had told me Lord Brackenfort's bedroom

was on the top level of the two-story home. Naturally. Because the first level would have been too easy.

Theus had warned the house might have additional alert systems in place for unauthorized intruders and quite probably shields to stop physical entry as well. So my basic plan was to climb up the outside wall, peek into his bedroom window to identify him, and do what I needed without setting foot inside. Easy, right?

I made it to the wall with only several scratches and a throbbing bruise on my shin from when my toes had found nothing but my swinging leg had found a great deal more.

So far so good.

I was relieved to find the wall was constructed of stone with sufficient toe and handholds for climbing. Especially since it was taller than I'd expected. The two stories must have had very lofty ceilings.

I was less pleased to find a familiar vine growing up its rough-hewn surface. The same one that had decorated our dorm room window in Millicent. It featured jagged six-sided leaves and blood-red thorns the length of my fingers.

I breathed in the sweet night air and readied myself. Then peered up the wall, chose a path that would let me avoid the vine for most of my ascent, and started climbing.

Halfway up, Gus's scornful voice broke into my mind and almost startled me into losing my grip.

I think this might be a new low even for you. Climbing the walls of some rich lordling like a common-born criminal.

"I *am* common born," I pointed out under my breath. "That hasn't been considered an insult for decades."

I climbed a bit farther.

"But I guess it might be a new low for you."

Gus sniffed.

For all his haughtiness, I'd brought him with me for good reason. Professor Cricklewood had made sure I wound up with a sword that had a unique ability to cut through magic. And while I was pretty sure this *wasn't* what Cricklewood had had in mind, if Lord Brackenfort had a magic shield I needed to break through, Gus would do the job.

Even if he did it with copious amounts of condescension and complaint.

In my distraction, I missed the young tendril of vicious vine hiding on a section of gently jutting stone and impaled my finger on one of its thorns.

Thinking curse words with great vehemence, I sucked my finger to stop the blood from dripping, stuck some sealing goop over it that I'd nicked from the base supplies, then snapped off the offending piece of vine and pocketed it (where it would quite likely stab me several more times before the night was done). Theus and Lirielle had warned me to leave no trace of my blood on Lord Brackenfort's property.

Magic was carried in the blood. Which meant magic could find and track blood. No need to leave a calling card.

I was only a few feet from the window ledge I was aiming for now. Which was just as well because my adrenaline was no longer offsetting my fatigue from the Malus drain. I should have hunted for some life force to supplement my own, but I'd had some vague notion of keeping my intake to a minimum in an attempt to keep my withdrawal to a minimum.

I urged my trembling limbs upward and hoped my shortsightedness wouldn't lead to disaster. I had no idea how many more times I'd have to climb up walls to peer into windows until I found the right one. Lirielle might have known his bedroom was on the second floor, but not *where* on the second floor.

My fingers found the window ledge. I eased my head up over the sill and peered into the dark room.

I couldn't see squat.

Cursing my inability to use my second sight until I'd confirmed the identity and was ready to strike, and hoping my target wasn't an insomniac staring out the window, counting imaginary shapeshifters, I climbed higher and pressed my face against the glass, trying to see inside.

I could just make out the shadowy shape of a bed. But whether it was Lord Brackenfort's bed or one for guests, and whether there was someone in it or it was unoccupied, I couldn't see well enough to tell.

Damn.

Then two things happened at once. The sentient home, either trying to aid me or knock me to my death, opened the awning window. And warm light spilled out into the darkness on the glass side of the home.

Double damn.

I flailed, scrabbling to dodge the swinging pane and regain my grip on the wall, found purchase, and froze. I waited for a shout, a magical attack, *something*.

But instead came the sound of a door opening and a flurry of rustling noises from something moving through the garden.

Then an older male voice said, "I told you, Fenris, no one's here. Or is your bladder getting as demanding as mine?"

Fenris? Who was Fenris?

A pet?

Did walkers *have* pets?

The rustling was getting closer, like whatever it was might be following my scent trail. And my brain began vividly conjuring images of giant hellhounds and a myriad of other monstrosities.

I glanced at the garden below, still unable to see what was coming, and back to the open window.

I chose the window.

Rushing to free Gus from his scabbard, I thrust him inside first, hopefully cutting through any magic wards. Then I scrambled in behind him.

The house helpfully turned on the lights, just long enough for me to see the perfectly made bed and deduce this was not Lord Brackenfort's room. Not unless he hadn't even been to bed. Or the bed made itself. Or—

I hissed, "Lights off," and the house obliged. Then I waited, heart thudding, to hear my downfall and the end of this midnight jaunt.

But again there were no cries of alarm or shouts of outrage or menacing threats. Which was almost worse. Either the old walker's hearing wasn't as good as others I knew, or he was feigning ignorance while setting a nasty trap for his home invader.

And I still didn't dare to use my magic to learn which. Not until I'd identified him or absolutely had to. Because surprise and secrecy were my best bets.

If Lord Brackenfort saw me, it was all over. Even if I won the exchange, the council would only be too happy for the excuse to order my execution. So to save myself, I'd be forced to kill Lord Brackenfort or... what?

I tiptoed across the plush rug, praying it wouldn't come to that, and cracked open the door. It swung ajar as silently as I could've hoped. Light was spilling up from below, and I could see the second story was not a whole second floor but a sort of loft taking up only half the house. The other half opened directly down into the grand glass-fronted living area. And I could see the back of a figure standing in the doorway, looking out into the garden. Where Fenris had apparently gone.

Unfortunately the likeness Perridor had provided to identify Lord Brackenfort hadn't featured the back of his head.

So I sank back into the meager shadows and lowered myself to the floor until I could see only the top of Brackenfort's head. Then I finally used magic.

Just a touch.

To knock a book from the shelf on one side of the living area.

The figure spun to look, no doubt both the noise and the magic alarm jangling in his awareness. But his gaze picked out the toppling book rather than my still form hidden in the shadows.

Target confirmed.

I hadn't expected that target to be awake of course. But with Ellbereth's magic at my disposal, it was not difficult to reach out and break his skin with an imagined pin. No more than a mosquito bite.

He slapped at his neck but did not realize the significance of that small sting, still searching for the intruder.

And then drinking in his life force was easy. Far too easy. No wonder the walkers were scared of me.

I used my second sight to carefully monitor his reserves. Watched him sway. And then with his life energy magnifying mine, making my movements impossibly fast, I leaped down the stairs to catch him as I drained him into unconsciousness.

I was gone, translocated through a gateway, before Fenris—whatever it was—had taken more than three bounding steps toward the house.

Lord Brackenfort's life energy sang in my veins as I alighted on the rocky perch where I'd left Theus and Lirielle. I felt myself smiling.

Mission accomplished. My debt had been repaid, and I'd gotten away free and clear.

I could be stupidly optimistic sometimes…

CHAPTER TWELVE

I slept fitfully, too full of Lord Brackenfort's life energy to require rest. Too guilty about what I'd done to enjoy the way the whole world felt clearer, brighter, more invigorating.

When I rose, the base seemed even starker in the dawn's light after experiencing the splendor of the walker city. But to keep pace with the Malus and minimize response time, the military bases were uprooted and repositioned every few months. Beautiful artistry was a luxury denied to the hollows.

I was heading to breakfast when Ellbereth caught me by the arm and dragged me into a quiet nook, her nails digging into my flesh.

She was the picture of fuming elegance. Her effortless ballet-dancer posture and graceful movements were precise with irritation, and her anger—

rather than contorting her pretty oval face and hazel eyes—only made them more becoming.

"Why did you use my magic last night?" she demanded.

In her current temper, her flame-red hair seemed to act as a warning beacon.

I didn't care.

"Because I had dire need," I told her. Because that was what we'd agreed on. I wouldn't use her magic unless I truly needed to.

"What need?" she hissed. "You were off duty. I checked. And I was already exhausted after whatever the hell you did when you were *on duty.*"

I extracted my arm from her grasp and borrowed a leaf from Lord Perridor's book.

"I never promised to explain my dire need to you. Only to refrain from using your magic unless I had one."

Her alabaster skin whitened further with the fury of someone unused to being denied. "I despise you."

"I hope you have a lovely day too," I said. Then I took pleasure, as I always did, in being able to turn my back on her and walk away unafraid.

The Reaper unit assembled in the mess hall for breakfast. Unit Commander Valesk was not a morning person, judging by her frown, but she was still turned out as meticulously as ever.

Actually, the frown had been there most of

yesterday too. Maybe she wasn't an *any* time of day person.

"The lord general wants us to try Nova's magic against the Malus again today," she said. "Except this time he wants her loaded with life force first. So we'll be going on a quick detour to undepleted territory."

We all understood what that meant.

Valesk's eyes shifted to Theus. "Then once we reach the perimeter, you will stay within reach of Armsman Nova at all times."

"Yes, sir."

"Be ready to depart in twenty minutes."

I was relieved we would be leaving so soon. The time lag before a withdrawal hit varied and could incapacitate me at the worst possible moment. At least this way I wouldn't drop in the middle of a mission and raise a whole bunch of questions I didn't want to answer.

"Yes, sir," we all chorused, and Valesk snatched up a seed-and-nut bar and left the rest of us to it.

I grazed on my own breakfast and observed my new unit members with interest.

Orlandrus and Dax *were* morning people. Which meant they made a lot of jokes, regaled us with highly embellished stories, and arranged their food into crude pictures that made them snicker before eating it.

Silvyr decidedly wasn't a morning person. His dirty-blond hair was rumpled from sleep rather than design, and his sparkling personality was on low wattage. But I did catch him sneaking Griff pieces of smoked fish.

I gave Griff the delicacies from my own plate and wondered if griffins could get fat.

Helena, the healer with over thirty years on the frontline, shook her head disapprovingly at one of Dax's jokes and then proceeded to tell the crudest joke of all. Noticing my astonishment, she said, "What? If one has to hear jokes over breakfast, they should at least be good ones."

Xanther ate in the silent, efficient manner in which he did everything else, but sat until the last of us was done.

Fletcher contributed little, keeping his attention on his food and occasionally stealing glances at Ameline or me. But I was glad to at least see him smile at some of the jokes.

I jogged to catch up with him as everyone left. We didn't have long, but I'd wanted to talk with him last night before everything had gone wrong with the Malus and then Perridor had called in his favor. And with withdrawal looming in my future, this might be the best opportunity I got for a while.

"Fletch, I…"

What should I say? What could I say?

"I missed you," I finished lamely.

The truth was I still missed him.

Once, he would have grinned easily in response to that statement, pulling me into a one-armed hug and ruffling my hair. "You know if you ever want to see me," he'd have said, "all you need to do is lean out your window and throw rocks at mine." It was true too. I'd kept a bowl of gravel and small shattered pieces of concrete that I'd collected around the city for just that purpose. And then we'd sneak out our respective bedrooms and meet by the palm tree on the corner.

Now he eyed me warily. "I'm sorry, Nova. I don't think I can do this."

"Do what?" I asked with a lightness I did not feel. "Have a conversation?"

What terrible thing had happened to him that he was so changed by this war? Because I was certain something must have. How else could Orlandrus and Dax and Silvyr and Helena and so many others retain a sense of humor, a zest for life? While my dear friend —whose warmth and welcome and kindness had extended to everyone, whose smile had made the world brighter, and whose presence had always assured me that everything would be okay—was unrecognizable.

"It's different out here," he said. "Caring too much is a liability."

He wouldn't meet my eyes, and it hurt to hear him say those words. Fletcher who had been the king of caring, who had always been there when I needed him, who had never turned anyone away.

Until now.

"I know I transferred to be part of your unit, but"—he paused and I waited, throat and chest aching with anticipation—"it wasn't for the friendship we once shared."

His tone was apologetic yet entirely unyielding.

"It's because I'm hoping you might put an end to this. I always knew you were special, and I guess I wanted to experience that hope firsthand."

"Ah," was all I managed in response. My eyes burned, but I was desperate not to let the tears fall.

"I'm sorry," he offered again. "But it's better this way. Out here relationships do more harm than good."

I wanted to argue. How many times had my friends saved my life at the academy? How much stronger was I for having them around me? Hell, even the Lord General Zaltarre recognized the value of relationships. That was why he preferred his armsmen to work in fixed units, why he'd ensured my friends formed part of mine.

Yet how could I gainsay Fletcher, who had survived out here two years, when this was only my second day? And wasn't this the same thing I was doing with Theus? Holding back to prevent the harm outweighing the good?

But that was different. Wasn't it?

I wasn't pushing away our friendship. Merely preventing it from going any further. And *I* was almost certainly going to die.

Oh.

That meant forcing my friendship on Fletcher was probably a selfish thing to do.

So I gave my old friend, the boy next door, or what was left of him, a weak attempt at a perky salute and let his stride outpace mine.

CHAPTER THIRTEEN

I didn't have time to grieve, and I was grateful for that. But I was nervous about how my new teammates would react to a display of my unique magic.

All morning I'd made an effort to move at what felt like a snail's pace to conceal the fact I was already high on extra energy. And now I was going to have to "hunt" in front of them.

No one had been any worse than neutral about my wildcard gift so far, but *seeing* my magic in action was different to just hearing about it. It would be impossible for them not to notice the similarities between my reaper magic and the enemy's that had caused so much sorrow and death.

At least I could take life energy without killing the donor.

Ameline and Bryn must have picked up on my nerves because they made an effort to distract me.

"Oh my gosh," Bryn gushed, "you should've seen Ellbereth come in after her first time on blazer duty. She's probably never been so dirty in her life, and I swear the layer of soot coating her skin *still* wasn't as black as her expression."

Bryn laughed wickedly, and I couldn't help smiling too.

Ameline shook her head in Bryn's direction. "You didn't look much better last night after your first game of Blob Blast. That black muck gets everywhere."

"Just because *you* were too chicken to play."

I'd sat out too, conserving my energy for Lord Perridor's favor. The game was sort of like a base version of dodgeball, with a hundred globular black blobs the size of watermelons floating around inside a glowing hexagonal enclosure. The blobs exploded in a shower of black gunk if they touched contestants anywhere but on their hands and feet, and the aim was to destroy all the blobs while remaining as clean as possible. No magic allowed.

No one had stayed wholly clean.

"I'd rather be a chicken than look like a swamp monster," Ameline retorted.

By now we were all grinning, and I felt a surge of love and gratitude for my friends. Who would the past six months have turned me into without their support? It wasn't just my physical life they'd saved.

I determinedly *didn't* think of Fletcher.

98

Silvyr looked more like his usual self when we met again for the mission.

"If you need a suggestion for a hunting ground, my friend in the Fleetfox unit mentioned a pack of harbinger jackals have been harassing our warren of skyfuries. Perhaps you could help dissuade them?"

I looked to our unit commander for approval. It seemed as good an idea as any. A way I could drain life force from other beings and be helpful at the same time. And at least the jackals would make for less embarrassing pest control opponents than snails.

Valesk shrugged. "So long as we don't waste time tracking them down. The lord general considers our mission as critical."

I noted Valesk said nothing about her own opinion on the import of my wildcard gift. But perhaps that was because to her it didn't matter. She might be abrupt and display all the warmth of an ice serpent, but she appeared utterly committed to carrying out her orders, regardless of her personal feelings about them.

Little wonder she expected absolute obedience from her own unit.

A few gateways later, we were standing in a hot and humid tropical forest before an intricate towering structure that looked like a luxury man-made cat tree on steroids. Two hundred feet worth of steroids.

Skyfuries scampered and flitted in and out of the myriad of openings in chittering mischief. Despite their name, the creatures were ridiculously cute and had a long-standing symbiotic relationship with world walkers. They looked kind of like ferrets, with long, slinky bodies and cone-shaped noses, except their ears were large and foxlike, they possessed functional feathered wings, and both fur and feathers came in the entire gamut of colors.

The creatures had historically been used sort of like humans had used messenger pigeons except with more mutual benefit and understanding. Sure walkers could just translocate to relay a message, but not every message required or wanted social interaction. So skyfuries had carried them in exchange for a life of safety filled with their favorite things, and they were affectionately referred to by many as sky*furries*.

Several of the more curious residents flew down to inspect us. A small fluffy specimen—with a yellow face that morphed into orange halfway down its body before darkening again to red—tried to land on Ameline's head but spotted Griff at the last moment. Chittering reproachfully, it swerved and changed trajectories to land on Bryn instead.

Yep, they were proper cute.

A predominantly white skyfury whose paws, ears, and tail looked like they'd been dipped in blue ink landed on me and sniffed my hair. This close, I could see the needle-like fangs that were the real reason for the *fury* part of their name.

Silvyr switched back to tour-guide mode. "This

warren regularly works with those on watch duty by doing sky patrols around the periphery of the Malus. Some things are easier to see by air, and these guys are fast and nearly tireless, with keen eyes and sharp minds that can relay what they see to anyone with the ability to communicate with them. Plus these guys now understand several dozen words in human dialects."

The one on my shoulder stood on its hind legs and scratched its chest as if proud of this achievement.

Silvyr went on, pausing only to rub a new arrival under the chin. It nipped him for his impudence, but delicately.

The bite still drew blood.

"They're smart, fast, and have impressive bite force for their size, but the harbinger jackals hunt the skies in packs with vicious cunning. In a one-on-one encounter, a skyfury will outmaneuver a jackal nineteen times out of twenty, but with the jackals hanging around the warren, those odds are too high. Not to mention—"

"This isn't an educational tour, Armsman Silvyr," Valesk interrupted. "How do we draw the jackals out?"

Silvyr ducked his head sheepishly. "Yes, sir. Ameline, you're good with animals, right? Can you explain what we're here for and ask a bunch of the skyfuries to fly from the warren at once but stay nearby? That should tempt the jackals into revealing themselves."

Ameline drew her bow. "Once this starts, the jackals are going to fall fast. Do we have a way of preventing them from breaking bones or wings when they hit the ground?"

A few of the walkers volunteered to be on "catch" duty. And then the skyfuries exited the protection of their tower en masse, chittering their defiance to the forest.

The harbinger jackal pack must indeed have been hanging around, because it took only seconds for them to appear. They were similar in appearance to the jackals indigenous to earth, except huge black glossy wings like a raven's sprouted from their shoulders and their claws were akin to talons suitable for rending and carrying prey.

The jackals worked together to herd or corner or scare their target into a pack mate's jaws or claws. But today they didn't stand a chance.

Ameline loosed arrow after arrow in quick succession, using skill and her bow's magic to ensure the arrowhead only ever hit her desired target.

She did not miss.

Each arrow grazed jackal fur or black wing enough to draw blood but not enough to do permanent damage. Theus and Lirielle, just as well-practiced, used magic to slice into others. And in my second sight I watched the jackals' life forces brighten and become accessible to me.

Six bolder members of the pack recognized the

threat and came at us, but Bryn deterred them with a wall of flame and a few singed noses.

It took only seconds for me to drain every one of the forty-three jackals to complete exhaustion and send them plummeting from the skies.

I hadn't even needed to take a single step.

Silvyr, Xanther, and Orlandrus softened their landings, Theus and Lirielle catching any they missed. And the chittering skyfuries dove down after them and sank their needle teeth into the downed predators as an added reminder to leave their territory.

Between Lord Brackenfort and the jackal's stolen life force, I knew I would be wretchedly ill with withdrawals later. Not to mention they'd be even worse if I actually succeeded with the Malus today.

But the regret of withdrawals felt a small world away right then.

Every cell and nerve ending was alive and singing, every sense amplified, and the air itself felt fresher and more life-giving. The rest of the world seemed to slow as my own awareness and movement sped up. More so again than after Lord Brackenfort's energy alone. And I knew my strength and athleticism was far greater too.

At least I wouldn't have to conceal my speed now that I had a publicly acceptable reason for it.

I glanced at my new teammates, suddenly afraid of what I'd find on their faces. But there was only wary respect in Silvyr's, Xanther's, and Helena's, the usual frown of concentration on Valesk's, and hope on Fletcher's.

Orlandrus and Dax were looking at me like I'd just done a party trick.

All were better than fear or loathing.

Good.

A shiver of exhilarated anticipation rippled through my supercharged body.

"I'm ready."

CHAPTER FOURTEEN

I should've felt fear as I faced down the Malus for the second time. Watching its black advance tendrils floating across the long-abandoned town Zaltarre had chosen for this confrontation. But I felt too vibrant, too powerful, too *alive* to feel fear.

This time *I* was going to rip life force from the Malus, and then perhaps I'd use its own life force, its own strength and power, to rip more.

A quiet voice told me I was being overconfident, but it was drowned out by the buzzing in my veins.

I caught myself baring my teeth in a feral grin. I seemed to do that a lot when I was supercharged on life force.

Theus stood beside me, his shoulder as close as it could be without touching, and I briefly wondered whether his magic would be able to contain mine when I was in this state.

The rest of the team were arrayed in defensive positions around us. Which was unnecessary, although I had Valesk's measure enough that I did not bother to protest. But if the Malus sent another dozen Taken our way, I could down them in seconds.

Still, I supposed I should shut my eyes.

Even my second sight was amplified. The Malus appeared brighter, yet my "vision" adjusted faster and I could more easily distinguish the life force of the beings it had yet to finish assimilating.

Bryn risked Valesk's displeasure to say, "Kick some black blobby butt, Nova."

And then, without further delay, I latched onto the Malus's life force and yanked.

We'd decided a short, hard tug would be best, draining the Malus before it could gather its full strength to retaliate. Maybe even before it realized what was happening.

Theus would then break contact.

So that's what I did, yanking as hard as possible with every ounce of my magnified force.

Power flooded into my already supercharged body, and I bit back a manic laugh. Then I felt the Malus react and blindly grabbed Theus's arm as we'd agreed.

Disorienting blackness.

Several muttered oaths.

And then a cheer from my teammates.

I opened my eyes in time to see what looked like a shower of black ash drifting to the ground, and the haze of the Malus cleared for about a mile all around us.

Theus freed his arm from my grasp, and my second sight confirmed what my eyes were seeing. The Malus's life force in our immediate vicinity had vanished.

No, not vanished.

Poured into me.

And I'd survived. I felt good. Great even. I had just enough time to feel hope. To think maybe this was actually possible…

And then my ears picked up a low hissing wail, and the ground where the Malus dust had so recently fallen began to tremble.

"Shield nets, now!" Valesk snapped.

I dove to the old cracked and buckled asphalt and activated my shield net, watching anxiously for each one of my unit members to catch up and do the same. In three seconds flat, the wailing escalated to deafening levels. The magic roared like it was a new monster come to life, picking up anything it could get its hands on and flinging them toward the seething darkness of the Malus. A trash can flew past, mere inches from my face, and an old A-frame slammed into Valesk's shield net, but her look of concentration did not change.

The magic roared louder. The hideous wailing a constant undercurrent. And I began to fear the asphalt beneath us wouldn't hold.

A rusted bus bounced past before taking to the air. An object surely never meant to fly. My view was almost completely obscured with flying debris and dirt and the constant barrage of airborne projectiles.

Buildings tore and toppled, the screech of rending metal audible even over the howling magic. Debris pelted my shield net, and a huge chunk of scaffolding bounced directly on top of Bryn's prostrated form. Incredibly, the shield nets' protections held, and I silently blessed the magic of the walkers.

Then, as abruptly as it had begun, the roar of power fell to silence, the dust and the debris that blocked out the sky settled once more into rest, and Valesk recalled her shield net.

The rest of us followed suit and looked around in gaping astonishment. Or at least us newbies did. The outskirts of the town Zaltarre had chosen for its defensible position was unrecognizable.

Entire buildings lay flattened, collapsed and scattered like a child's wooden blocks after a tantrum. The road had been transformed from clear footing for combat to a minefield of tripping hazards. In mere minutes, the town that had stood strong through years of neglect and abandonment had been ripped apart.

The destruction was worse immediately around us, making it clear who the Malus had been targeting. But even streets away roofs had been torn off and trees toppled.

"Basilisk's balls," Bryn breathed into my ear via the

squeaker. "I don't think the Malus appreciates getting a taste of its own medicine."

But the Malus wasn't done.

A small army of Taken emerged from the encroaching darkness. Not a mere dozen like the day before. I counted at least fifty with more still appearing.

No… They were not Taken.

I glanced at my more experienced teammates and was unreassured by their expressions of consternation.

This was new then.

Unseen in 150 years of war.

Valesk began quietly relaying what we were seeing to Lord General Zaltarre.

"They're like rough-hewn golems ranging from ten to thirty feet tall and made of something like black stone. No weapons but they don't look as if they'll need them. And the Malus is following right on their heels."

It was an accurate description of what they looked like, but I saw more. These were not mere inanimate objects constructed of available materials and magically given the *appearance* of life. They had their own life force, a part of the Malus's and yet distinct. And their physical forms were vague distorted echoes of what they had once been. Before the Malus had ripped them from those lives forever. As if a part of them remembered.

In many, the life force of multiple creatures had

merged together, creating strange new mishmashes of monsters. A dragon's sinewy neck and powerful head was stuck sideways on a dire wolf's body, and the thing had the tails of both. A dread bear sported a grotesque skirt of writhing limbs. Another creature had more heads than legs.

But whatever they were, and whatever they'd once been, they still embodied the Malus's intent.

Attack.

A half mile out, Valesk gave the order. "Reaper unit, commence long-range assaults."

Someone, probably Dax, struck the leading monster with a bolt of lightning. The elephantine-kraken thing did not even slow. Bryn unleashed a fireball on the same monster, engulfing it in flame that did not die. But again, the elephantine-kraken mash-up did not react, and when Bryn let the flames extinguish a minute later, it didn't even have the decency to smoke.

Issuing a quick warning to my unit, I tried pitting the Malus's own magic against the monsters. The vortex power I'd drawn from the Malus's life force cut a deep furrow into the earth at their feet and whipped the soil and rocks into a frenzy around them, but the beings themselves were unaffected.

Attempting to flood their minds with fear was equally fruitless.

The other walkers in my unit focused on their own

attacks, but whatever they did was invisible to me and had no impact on the oncoming force.

Valesk's next report to Zaltarre was more grim. "They appear to be impervious to magical attack. We may require reinforcements."

Zaltarre's reply was delayed. "Hold tight, Reapers. We're rousing all off-duty units, but the other teams on the perimeter are having troubles too."

A quarter mile out, Ameline, having no magic to fling at them, nocked an arrow and let it fly. They were still too far away for accuracy, but there were so many of them and they were so large it was almost hard to miss. Her arrow took one of the creature's in a giant knee and the monster stumbled. There was no cry of pain, no flinch or other normal reaction, but the leg dragged now, obviously damaged.

They *could* be harmed then.

I bounced on my toes, wanting to rush forward and put Gus and my amplified speed, strength, and skill to the test. But I was supposed to be working as part of a unit. "Permission to advance, Unit Commander?"

"Hold the line, Armsman. Let them expend the energy coming to us. No point doing the Malus's work for it."

Ameline shot more arrows into them, concentrating her attention on those with only two legs so she could ensure they never reached us. Helena joined her as soon as they were in crossbow range. And the walkers shifted to indirect methods of magic attack, flinging heavy or sharp, jagged chunks of debris at them.

The sharp, cutting debris worked better. The Echoes—as we decided to designate them—were tough and could bat away a flying hunk of concrete like it was no more than a pillow.

My stolen vortex power was too imprecise to do much good. So I waited uselessly, quivering like a restrained hunting hound.

It seemed to take an age for the Echoes to cross the last quarter mile, but in reality it was probably only a minute. They were running or galloping or going whatever flat-out pace they could manage with their messy assemblage of limbs. And the towering darkness of the Malus was still right on their heels.

Then—finally—Valesk said, "Give them hell, armsmen."

And I shot forward into the melee to greet them with Gus's lethal edge.

I had just enough time to lop off the first monster's head—just enough time to see that two-thirds of the Echoes were coming specifically at me—before the Malus swept forward.

And then we were swallowed by darkness and choking fear.

We had trained for this. Trained so that we would not lose our will, our nerve, would not crumple before the onslaught of a fear so powerful that it could make you forget your own existence. Could make you forget the existence of anything except the soul-crushing, smothering, suffocating, shattering suspension of all but terror.

And so I did not freeze. I did not lose all sense of self. I kept moving as my eyes adjusted to the lack of light, and my mind staggered under the weight of that savage fear.

I ran—blindly at first—trying to draw the bulk of the monsters away from my team and simultaneously make myself a difficult target. And as I ran, I ignored the part of my mind that was gibbering in terror and focused instead on the part of me that could still sort of see. My second sight.

The life force of the Echoes was harder to distinguish in the midst of the Malus's glaring light, but there, a striking serpentine neck, and there, a swipe of oversized claws. I spun and cut them down.

There was no scream, no grunt, no heavy breath, no spray of blood. The only way I knew I'd hit something was the sound and slight resistance as Gus cleaved their unnatural "flesh." Then the sight of their life force losing form and dissolving back into the Malus.

I reported that last detail through the squeaker. If the Malus was reclaiming the fallen monsters' energy, was there any point fighting these creatures?

The question did not stop me cutting the next Echo's five legs out from under it and cleaving through two necks of another.

Something smashed into the back of my unprotected head, pitching me forward into the oncoming strike of a tusked-gorilla thing. I flung myself sideways and managed—barely—to evade that second blow. But pain from the first ricocheted through my skull and blood ran warm and wet over my face and scalp.

Then my supercharged healing kicked in and the wound closed, the pain vanishing, leaving only the sticky blood behind.

Bryn's heatless flames pushed back the smothering black shroud of the Malus just enough that we could see vague outlines in the gloom. And I could identify the projectile that had landed next to me...

The reason I hadn't seen the blow coming with my 360-degree second sight was because it hadn't been one of the Echoes that had struck me. It had been a damned cement garden gnome with a demented grin on its chipped and faded face.

I shoved away from it to dodge the stomping mass of a huge stoneboar and flipped to my feet, my enhanced vision taking in the now semi-visible details of our surroundings.

Here inside the Malus, the debris it had ripped from that city was still swirling, giving our enemy plenty of ammunition. Attempting to wield my own vortex power against the debris only added to the chaos.

Bryn employed a more useful tactic and engulfed

each Echo in flames. Not to harm them, since that was impossible, but to make them stand out in the Malus's cloaking darkness.

And while Bryn pushed back the darkness, Ameline used her mind magic to push back the choking fear.

I didn't even realize how heavy that oppressive weight sat upon me until it was softened, edged back. Even though I hadn't frozen, hadn't run in terror, I also hadn't been anywhere close to giving it my all. The mental wrestle had been sapping my vigor, dividing my attention from the physical fight.

No longer.

I threw myself at the jostling monsters.

The Echoes had strength that surpassed even my own augmented power, but they weren't as fast. And I milked that advantage for all it was worth as I dodged flying debris, skull-crushing blows, and rending paws, maws, and talons to dart inside their longer reach and slash Gus across their vital parts.

Except determining *which* were the vital parts was a challenge in itself. Their bodies were not of flesh and blood, but lopping off heads, fighting limbs, or weight-bearing appendages all worked to neutralize them. The problem was if a beast had three heads, you had to lop off all three of them before it stopped attacking.

So I did. I dashed and darted and dodged and struck again and again, butchering our silent opponents with a ruthless efficiency and unnatural skill even Valesk couldn't frown at.

All the while I hoped my friends were safe. I tried and failed to confirm it with my own eyes, but I was hemmed in on every side by the monstrous Echoes. And as many as I felled, there were always more waiting for their chance to rend me into pieces.

The Malus was *creating* more.

Someone screamed. And kept screaming. A gut-wrenching sound that went on and on. Mercifully the squeaker knew not to relay *that* vocalization.

I couldn't tell who it was, but I knew it wasn't one of our eerily silent opponents. Fear squeezed my heart with icy fingers, and this time Ameline's mind shielding could not help because the fear came from within me.

Then the screaming stopped. Which was worse.

"Fletcher's down," Helena reported. Which meant his shielding magic that might have been protecting the others until now was down too. "It looks bad."

Valesk cursed. "Do what you can for him, Helena, then deploy his shield net. Orlandrus, Dax, protect her while she works."

With the worst of the fighting centered around me, I dared not get closer to my old friend. So I poured my fear and fury into a fresh frenzy of hacking at the enemies that surrounded us. They fell. But more replaced them. And though my body healed every wound I took, that magic was costly to my reserves of stolen life force.

I scaled the body of the tallest Echo trying to kill me, narrowly dodged the swing of a barbed tail, and looked into the murky darkness. I could make out only the vague outline of one figure huddling over a still, prostrate one.

Lord General Zaltarre spoke into our squeakers. "Backup units are ready for deployment, but I'm on the verge of ordering a mass retreat. Unless you have good news for me, Reaper unit?"

"No, sir, we're losing." Valesk's words held a bitter edge. "We've killed dozens of the bastards, but the Malus has made dozens more, and Armsman Nova reports the life force is being recycled rather than lost."

She paused, grunting as she presumably defended herself or someone else. "Also, based on the way they're concentrating around our wildcard, I don't think they'll stop till she's dead."

Zaltarre's voice was heavy. "Then get out of there, Reapers. And make it back to camp alive. That's an order."

Our chorus of "Yes, sirs" was weak.

CHAPTER FIFTEEN

We ran. But the Echoes ran too. And they were tireless. And fast.

Worse, while we were within the Malus's dark borders, it could form new monsters in our path and did so at alarming speeds.

"Gateway," Valesk ordered. "Short distances only."

Xanther seemed tireless too. He and I took the rearguard position without a word, fending off the Echoes from our companions as they dove through the gateway.

Silvyr was carrying Fletcher, and Helena ran beside them trying to keep her patient alive. Orlandrus was assisting a heavily limping Dax and opening the gateways. Valesk was trying to see everywhere at once, giving orders and providing backup wherever was needed. And Bryn and Ameline were putting everything they had left into running, shielding us from the fear, and lighting our way. A random corner of my brain noted Ameline's quiver was almost empty.

I was covered in my own blood but no longer wounded. I didn't think Xanther could say the same, but still he ran and fought without ceasing, making heavy use of his metal arm.

One gateway. Two. Three.

The darkness of the Malus seemed to go on and on. When had it advanced so far? How much farther did it continue?

"I didn't realize this was what all those morning runs were for, Commander," Silvyr puffed. "I thought you just wanted your team to look pretty."

Valesk declined to comment.

"At least this way if you fail to attract a partner, Silvyr, you can always chase one down," Orlandrus said helpfully.

Was the darkness becoming more transparent? Or was it only my outlook that had lightened?

"Griff says another few hundred yards and we'll be clear," Ameline reported.

Clear of the darkness where we might attempt some longer distance gateways. Where we might finally leave the Echoes behind. And then at last we might properly tend to Fletcher.

The view of his pale, lifeless face and the copious blood that had changed Silvyr's golden body armor to a slick red made my gut clench.

It didn't matter that he'd rejected my overtures of

friendship. It didn't matter that I was probably going to die in the next few months. I wanted Fletcher to live, dammit.

Another gateway. Another three Echoes down, another deep gash on my thigh, quickly healed. And finally we were free of the darkness. Free of the Echoes.

We went through three more short-distance gateways in quick succession, and there on the barren earth, Valesk deemed us safe enough to see to Fletcher.

He looked so much worse than seven minutes ago when we'd started our retreat.

Silvyr laid him gently on the lifeless soil, revealing the deep lacerations across his abdomen that would've cut him in half had it not been for the body armor taking the brunt of the blow. But even the walker-strengthened body armor had failed.

It was a mercy he was unconscious.

I hissed in a breath, my vision blurring.

Helena knelt and laid her hands on his undamaged shoulders.

I couldn't breathe. Ameline took my hand, and I was pretty sure she wasn't breathing either. We waited for the torn organs to make themselves whole again. The surrounding flesh to knit back together. Perhaps the color to return to his bloodless face.

But nothing happened.

Helena rocked back, her expression grim. "He doesn't have enough strength left to heal."

No. I shook my head.

No!

Fletcher couldn't die.

I stumbled to his side and fell heavily beside him, grabbing for the hand that had held mine so many times. His bigger one enveloping mine to lend me comfort and strength. My first day of community school when I was five. The first time I'd dared to venture to the edge of the city. The many nights I'd snuck out and railed against my mother's apparent indifference to me or the injustice of the Firstborn Agreement. Even the night before he'd left when I'd tried and failed to hide my grief.

His hand was larger and rougher now with calluses it had once lacked. But it was still Fletcher's.

He couldn't die.

Except his life force thread was so fragile—as tattered and tenuous as a ruined butterfly wing.

It wasn't fair. I still had so much life force, and he was damn near empty. Too empty to heal.

He couldn't die.

The words thudded through me with every beat of my heart. *He can't die. He can't die. He can't die.*

But he was dying.

I tried to think. And then I stopped thinking and just acted. I had extra life force. He had too little. So I *shoved* my own life force at him. At his body where it would have been contained before the transformation ritual. At the tattered thread that led back to his supply in the human cache.

It felt similar but not the same as when the Malus had attempted to drain me dry. I could sense the life force dwindling, shifting, leaving, but I was in control. Sort of.

And then I wasn't.

Agony, hot and blinding, shredded my gut and I bit back a scream, but only barely. I was whimpering. Tears were running down my cheeks. But I could see life force surrounding and filling Fletcher.

Was this excruciating pain what he was feeling? Or would be if he'd been conscious?

Ameline, who'd come to kneel beside Fletcher too, fluttered her hands over my face, then yanked up my shirt and body armor to access my stomach that I hadn't realized I'd been clutching.

"Nova, what's wrong?"

"Try. Again," I ground out, curling into a fetal position like it might relieve this invisible agony.

Unable to see what I could, but trusting me, Ameline whirled to Helena.

"You heard her. Try again. Please."

Helena's voice was tired, resigned. "There's no use—"

"Nova's gift is all about transferring life force. It will cost you nothing to try!"

"I'll do it." That was Lirielle.

I barely heard them through the pain, but I

focused on keeping a steady stream of life force flowing into Fletcher's ruined body.

And then I heard gasps of astonishment, Ameline's cry of hope, and I prayed it would be enough, that I could give enough to heal his otherwise lethal wounds.

It hurt too much to push myself up to see for myself.

"Let me take over," Helena whispered.

Theus was hovering over me. Perhaps wanting to touch me, comfort me, but scared to. Scared of breaking my magic connection with Fletcher.

Slowly, so, so slowly, the agony lessened. Was I getting used to it? Was I growing numb? Or... was Fletcher being healed?

"It's working," Theus whispered to me, sensing my need to know. So I kept pouring. And then the pain eased enough that I could look up.

The bone-deep lacerations had transformed into pink rigid scars. Fletcher's eyes were still shut, but he was breathing slowly and deeply as if in sleep. No longer the shallow uneven breaths that had so scared me.

Helena shifted her eyes from her patient to me, and for the first time I saw actual hope in her eyes. "Do you know how much good you could do as a healer?"

Then withdrawal hit, and I collapsed into a darkness I could not fight and Bryn's fire could not light.

CHAPTER SIXTEEN

If only I had hung on a little longer, I might have saved more lives than Fletcher's that day.

Reports trickled in over the next hours of the damage and casualties the Malus's revenge had wrought. Because of me. Because I'd ripped one lousy square mile of the Malus's life force.

The cost was far too high.

Even without the withdrawal, I would've felt sick to my stomach over it. But the withdrawal was brutal. The worst I'd ever experienced.

I vomited repeatedly until I began to fear my gut was as shredded as Fletcher's had been. The violent spasms sent fresh waves of fire through every part of my already wretchedly miserable body. And when the spasms released me to slump back against the mattress, the soft sheets scraped my skin like Ellbereth was attempting to flay me with a blunted eating knife while I wasn't looking.

With my eyes scrunched shut against the pain of opening them, I would've been an easy target.

Except Ameline and Bryn stayed with me. As they always did. Ameline tending to my every need and murmuring soothingly that it would be over soon, everything would be all right, and something about Theus standing outside the door, but not to worry, she wouldn't let him in until I was feeling better.

"Maybe wait until she's smelling better too," Bryn put in helpfully from across the room where she'd been pretending to polish her axe for at least an hour.

And Ameline murmured even more gently that we ought to put stinkwort in Bryn's shampoo.

Hours passed in this fashion, each one a little less torturous than the last. But when I was finally well enough to form coherent thoughts and possibly even verbalize them, guilt swamped me.

"I've made everything worse," I croaked.

Bryn snorted. "Only because you made the Malus feel *threatened* for the first time in 150 years. That's got to mean something!"

"People died, Bryn."

"People are always dying," she said matter-of-factly. "And unless we can do a great deal more than make the Malus *feel* threatened, we're all going to join them in a few short years."

Ameline, dear sweet Ameline who cared more

deeply for others' suffering than anyone else I knew, said, "Bryn's right. You aren't doing anyone—dead or alive—any favors if you sit on your hands and try nothing. Even if trying new things puts others at risk."

The weight of those words landed like bricks and sat just as heavy.

"So what do I try next?" I asked quietly.

Bryn chewed her lip. "Doesn't your sword have any suggestions? He's seen thousands of battles, hasn't he?"

"Yes. He suggested I try to avoid dying."

Bryn snorted. "I think even Choppy could've come up with that."

Gus sniffed. *It's sound advice.*

Ameline put her hands on her hips. "I think if you're going to beat yourself up and work yourself into a state of distress, you should at least finish recovering from withdrawal first. Also, there's some people who want to see you, and if you're up to it, I'll help you into the shower before I let them in. You're covered in… um, blood from the fight."

"Oh sure, it's the blood that's the worst thing on her," Bryn said. "I'll fetch some new bedding."

The first of my visitors was Theus.

"Your friends can be very bossy sometimes," he informed me.

The friends in question had gone to find something to eat where the smell wouldn't affect my still queasy stomach.

"They wouldn't let me in earlier."

"Consider it a kindness," I advised. "To both of us."

His lips twitched. "Oh? Do you get very cranky when you're ill?"

Mine twitched too. "Viciously so, I'm afraid. I'm like a werewolf having a bad fur day."

Theus for some reason I didn't understand had taken a recent interest in human fantasy fiction. Maybe they read like comedy to him.

In any case, he laughed now. A rich, delightful sound that sent a tingle down my spine.

Then he gazed at me with those deep, deep green eyes of his, and the tingle turned into something warmer.

Tentatively he reached out and pushed my still damp hair from my face. "I think I'd like to see that someday…"

The door swung open, and Theus's hand and gaze left me.

I regretted the loss of both more than I cared to admit.

"Oh, hello, Wildcard," Lirielle said. Her tone was one of absent, mild surprise, as if she could've found anyone in my sleeping quarters and it was merely a stroke of good fortune that it was me.

And Theus.

For someone with prophetic powers, Lirielle had rotten timing.

She drifted across the room, fingers trailing languidly along the wall, then stopped abruptly and fixed her smoky blue stare on me. "I have a new message for you."

Oh boy. That meant the future-predicting variety. Out of the handful she'd given me, only one of them had sounded positive, and that one had backfired big time.

"Prepare yourself," Lirielle intoned with an intensity that belied her usual dreamy manner. "Before your power shakes the worlds, you yourself will first be shaken."

Well didn't that sound flipping wonderful? I knew from experience there was no point asking for clarification. Her answers always wound up confusing me more. But the basic meaning of this one was clear enough.

I wanted to curse my "gift," but my next visitor the door opened itself for stopped the words from forming.

Fletcher.

He was standing like it hurt to fully straighten, but he was alive. Upright. And for some reason I couldn't guess, *here*.

"May I come in? Or I can come back after—"

"No." Theus and I interrupted simultaneously.

"Come in," I added.

Fletcher did so, his steps stiff and stilted. Theus pulled an armchair up for him—which Fletcher sank into with obvious relief—and then Theus silently left the room. Lirielle floated out after him.

Alone with my childhood friend, I felt irrationally nervous.

"Helena told me what you did for me."

"I would have done the same for anyone," I told him quickly. And then I realized how that sounded and added, "You don't owe me anything."

"At the very least," Fletcher said, "I owe you an explanation."

"You really don't—"

He held up his hand. "I want to. Look, I won't go into details, but during my time at the Firstborn Academy, I made a new friend. A good one. And when we both ended up in Raptor unit, I was stoked."

He shifted in the armchair like he couldn't find a position that didn't hurt.

"About ten months later, our unit got into a bad situation. One of our teammates was seriously hurt—fatally, although I didn't know it at the time—and my unit commander ordered a retreat. I didn't listen. Disobeyed. I thought I could save the downed teammate, and my friend stayed with me to protect my back."

Fletcher swallowed and continued bitterly.

"Two of our unit members died that day when it

should've been one. Because I was naive. Because I cared too much. I made a mistake, and my friend paid for it with his life."

"I'm sorry."

I wanted to say more, but I didn't think he'd hear me. Not in a way that would make a difference.

He shook his head. "That's not the part I came here to tell you." He swallowed again. "I know this is cliché, but when I believed I was dying today, I realized that punishing myself for one mistake is not how I want to live. It certainly isn't how Paul would've wanted me to live."

He rubbed his face, looking more burdened than freed by this revelation.

"I don't even know what that looks like in practice," he admitted tiredly. "But I wanted to thank you for saving my life. I'll try to make it worth something."

Fletcher didn't hang around, and I didn't push him to. I was exhausted after my three visitors, still a long way off being fully recovered from the withdrawal.

But I couldn't rest. My mind churned over everything that had happened and everything that was yet to come.

Our second experiment with the Malus—that had for a brief moment seemed so promising—was a dead end. The cost was too high, the gain too small. All we'd done was prove that a direct assault against the enemy would never work. Not even if we broke it down into bite-sized pieces.

I had never truly expected it to.

The Malus was a helluva lot larger than an elephant after all.

It had devoured most of the life force from two worlds. Billions upon billions of living things that now gave it their strength, their life's energy.

Sure, the Malus had also depleted some of that energy to move, to fight, and to defend itself over the past 150 years, but I could never match its strength. Even if I were to somehow draw on the life force of every remaining being on our dwindling world, the Malus would have far more.

So in a battle of brute strength, even a long, drawn-out one, I was destined to lose.

And the cost of the Malus's retaliation was too damn high. We'd proven that today too.

Which meant we had to find a different approach. A less direct one. A *smarter* one.

If only I had any ideas about what that could be.

I remembered Lirielle's words.

Prepare yourself. Before your power shakes the worlds, you yourself will first be shaken.

I would've liked to believe she was referring to the withdrawal I'd just undergone.

But I wasn't that fortunate or that much of a fool.

CHAPTER SEVENTEEN

They came for me an hour before dawn. Two walkers who had the look and bearing of soldiers but were not hollows.

The overeager door to our sleeping quarters let them in when Millicent never would have.

"You need to come with us, Wildcard. We've been asked to escort you to the city."

I sat up in bed, disoriented after waking abruptly from a heavy, healing sleep.

"What? Why? And didn't you hear? It's not safe for you here. The Malus is restless and unpredictable right now."

"Then cooperate so we can depart shortly. Please remove any and all weapons on your person—"

"Not until you tell me what's going on."

I crossed my arms to shield myself from their

demands and scrutiny, glad I slept in our soft and wrinkle-resistant uniforms.

"Yes," Bryn put in, kicking her legs over the side of her own bed, closer to her battle-axe, I realized. "I'd like to know what's going on too." She shot a glance toward the still open door. "Ameline, get Theus and Lirielle. Maybe Valesk as well."

Ameline, her hair mussed and brow furrowed, rushed out.

The walker on the right was equal parts boredom and irritation. "This is a council matter, nothing to do with the hollow forces."

"I think you'll find Lord General Zaltarre will disagree with you on that," Bryn countered. "Anything that concerns Wildcard Nova concerns—"

"The lord general is aware we're here," said the same walker.

That was when I started to worry.

If the lord general had given them permission to escort—arrest?—me, that was bad news. *Really* bad news.

But I ignored my racing heart, hoping their keen senses wouldn't note the way it had just accelerated, and insisted, "Tell me what this is about."

The man on the left, who seemed a shade more empathetic than his partner, met my gaze. "Lord Brackenfort."

Crap, crap, crap.

The walker I'd drained. How much did they know?

It took me a beat too long to think to ask, "Who's that?"

I could see in the empathetic one's sapphire-blue eyes that he caught my hesitation. His face hardened.

"Cooperate and come with us, or we will have no other choice but to take you by force."

The other walker slid a case from his pocket and flipped it open just long enough for me to catch a glimpse of what was inside. Hells. A bloodjewel beetle. I *hated* bloodjewel beetles. I fought off a flashback of lying paralyzed and helpless at the bottom of the arena as the icy-cold water rose, covering my mouth, flooding my nostrils, stealing away the stars…

"All right, all right," I said.

If I was going to be dragged before the council, I'd prefer to be able to move my limbs while I was there. Not that I couldn't remove the bloodjewel pin with Ellbereth's magic, but revealing that ability could be even more disastrous than the Lord Brackenfort thing.

So despite Bryn's protests, I went with the walkers.

But not soon enough.

They led me through the first short-distance gateway, and that was when everything went wrong.

The walker on my left, the nicer one with sapphire-blue eyes, crashed into me.

I grunted a protest, then froze as I registered the meaning behind the clumsy, heavy weight of his body.

"Run," I snapped at the other walker.

My second sight showed what had been invisible in the dark. The advance tendrils of the Malus spreading around us.

And the walker who'd collapsed into me, already dead.

I shoved at his partner. "The Malus is here. *Run.*"

But what the hell was the Malus doing *here*? Why was it advancing into barren land?

Unless…

The second walker hesitated for a heartbeat, torn between the instinct to help his partner and the knowledge of imminent yet invisible danger.

Knowledge won, and he sprinted away from the Malus's encroaching grasp. Leaving me alone with the nicer walker, the one with the sapphire-blue eyes and a glimmer of empathy, lying motionless in the dirt.

I could see the bright light of his life force now captured within the Malus's never-ending reservoir. I didn't even know the walker's name. But his golden figure was still so perfectly formed, so whole and as yet uncorrupted by the Malus, that if I hadn't been standing over his lifeless body, I would've sworn he'd merely moved location.

Impulsively I pushed my life force at that glowing figure, kind of like I'd done for Fletcher. Maybe if I lent him my strength he could break free and return to his still-warm and waiting body?

Except the life force available to me was only mine

this time, and I was still recovering. Giving it away *hurt*.

All of a sudden I felt what the walker was feeling. Confusion. Disorientation. A sea of unintelligible voices and the power of the Malus tearing at him, scrabbling at the edges of his mind until it began to fray. And I could feel his fear of losing himself under the barrage of that onslaught.

But *he* was still in there, I realized in shock. The walker, whose name I now somehow knew was Vaegon. His mind, his will, his memories were still there.

And the power I was giving him was shoring him up, helping him hold on to that.

"Get out," I shouted.

Could he hear me? Was he aware of me as I was of him?

But his focus was arrested by his fleeing friend. And through my connection with Vaegon and my own second sight, I sensed the Malus reaching for the kill.

The second walker was opening a gateway, but he was going to be too slow, too late. He was going to die.

And I feared I would die with them, because my life energy was still feeding into Vaegon, and when I tried to stop, to break the connection, I found I couldn't.

The Malus wasn't *pulling*. Perhaps because I was

already giving it my energy. But I was weak and weakening. I'd fallen to my knees beside Vaegon's body, and I wasn't sure that I would ever rise.

I was a fool.

Then Vaegon did something new.

Like the Echoes, he was part of the Malus, yet distinct. But unlike the Echoes, he retained his own will.

And he used that will and the power I'd fed him to shove the reaching grasp of the Malus back. Away from his friend. Just for a second.

But a second was all his friend needed to dive through the gateway and snap it shut behind him.

The Malus lunged forward again, but there was nothing to grab.

I could feel how much that single moment of defiance had cost the walker. Had cost *us*. The blackness encroaching my vision now was not the darkness of night nor the fog of the Malus. But I could not stop the flow of my dwindling life energy into the walker with sapphire-blue eyes…

Then hands grabbed my shoulders and my second sight went dark. My sense of Vaegon severed.

"Nova?" The way Theus spoke my name made it clear it wasn't the first time he'd said it.

"I'm okay."

I tried to stand but couldn't. Vaegon's lifeless body was only inches from my bowed head, and my own body shook with shock.

Theus lifted me gently into his arms. "Sorry. I know you don't like being carried, but we need to get out of here before the Malus's Echoes show up."

"But…" My teeth rattled so hard it was an effort to speak. And the cogs of my brain were malfunctioning. Why was I thinking about the solid warmth of Theus's chest at a time like this? "I'm supposed to go to the council… I think they know about Lord Brackenfort."

"The council can wait," Theus said firmly. "We need to tell Zaltarre the Malus has breached the perimeter watch."

So I sank into the warm press of Theus's embrace and closed my eyes.

All too soon we arrived at the command headquarters. But my shock was wearing off, so when Theus rapped on the door and asked if I would like to try standing, I nodded. This time my legs held me.

Zaltarre already knew the Malus was on the move. A horrendous screeching alarm went off just as one of his aides opened the door, and his office was a storm of activity with people rushing around and speaking urgently into their specialized squeakers.

The fact that one of my escorts had been killed, however, was news to him. And not welcome news either.

Over the next few minutes, we learned that the lord general's intel about the breach had arrived only seconds before we did. Individuals who had the ability to see or sense the Malus in the dark were always limited, and after the disaster of yesterday with many injured and others dead, the perimeter watch had been stretched thin. Because of this, and because it had been stretched *especially* thin along the barren segment where there was little left to protect, the Malus had gotten farther than it should have before anyone raised the alarm.

"I believe it's targeting our bases for further retaliation," Zaltarre said, "so I'm ordering an evacuation. There's no point in defending barren land."

He spoke, as he always did, with a mixture of conviction, command, and focused intensity that made the listener want to jump to obey.

Then that intensity focused on me. And I felt the weight of his disappointment like a sky whale had fallen from the sky and chosen me for a landing spot.

"But it's best not to keep the council waiting," he said. "Especially if you require them to be merciful."

There was no anger in his words.

Which somehow made it worse.

His gaze swept over his hectic office and returned to me.

"My aides can handle the evacuation. I will escort you to the council myself."

CHAPTER EIGHTEEN

Somehow the walker city didn't hold quite the same charm for me on this occasion.

Lord General Zaltarre forbid any of my friends from following and escorted me to the Court of Hearing. The ominous structure was a raised circular platform that the supplicant or accused had to walk up an imposingly long steep staircase to reach.

"If the council members don't want to be kept waiting," I muttered, "perhaps they should make the court more accessible."

"You've already kept them waiting," Zaltarre replied. "It is possible to translocate directly to the dais, but I believe a show of respect may prompt some of the elder council members to look upon you more favorably."

Either Zaltarre was messing with me, something I

considered unlikely, or he was on my side. I took some small comfort in that.

But the comfort did not ease the burn of my heavily fatigued muscles. I'd yet to completely recover from the worst withdrawal I'd ever experienced, and then I'd gone and poured most of my life energy into Vaegon. I was exhausted on every level.

Okay, maybe Zaltarre wasn't messing with me. Maybe he was *punishing* me.

I almost wished I'd been stabbed with the blood-jewel beetle after all so I wouldn't have to walk.

We were over halfway up the stairs and the sky was lightening with the first rays of dawn before I could see more of what was waiting for me. Arranged in a semi-circle were seventeen chairs that looked for all the world like oversized thrones woven from living silver branches. Each "throne" sat upon its own small dais with its own set of stairs, and upon each of them was a walker.

That left me to stand below them in the center of the larger circular platform.

The effect was intimidating. I suspected it was meant to be.

All the better for them to look down on me with scorn and disapproval.

The lord general had stopped at the top of the stairs behind me. There were no chairs, not even ordinary ones, for non-council members.

One other person was left standing, and I could

guess her purpose for being here from Zaltarre's warning.

"They'll have a strong mind mage," he'd told me. "And while they can't rummage through your brain, they will be able to tell if you're lying and sometimes pick up on surface thoughts and stronger emotions."

I had no idea how to handle that. How could I do anything but lie when I had so many secrets to protect?

The mind mage was gorgeous but relatively plain by walker standards. She did not acknowledge my arrival as I passed her to stand in the center of the platform.

The council members themselves varied widely in age and appearance. But all of them were beautiful and dressed in finery that made Zaltarre's and my uniform feel shabby in comparison.

Lady Neryndrith was recognizable for two reasons. One, she had the same flame-red hair and perfect ballet-dancer posture as Ellbereth. Two, her gaze upon me was as glacial as the continent on which I'd irreversibly bound my life to her daughter's.

I shivered and looked away.

Lord Brackenfort, the man whose life force I'd drained, was sitting at the next throne over, his expression impressively bland all things considered. My cheeks flushed, and I passed over him quickly.

Lord Perridor was there in the semicircle too of course. I was cautious not to let my gaze linger any longer on him than all the other council members who were new to me.

Hemmed in on all sides by the stately, formidable figures, it was impossible not to be reminded that I was standing before seventeen of the most powerful walkers in existence.

The walker on the throne directly in front of me was the oldest of them all. He wore his steel-colored hair long but well-groomed, and his gnarled fingers were bedecked with jewels. He waved one glittering hand.

"Lady Chandrelle, if you would kindly demonstrate the thread."

"Of course," murmured a delicate, pretty woman with a complexion of burnt umber and beautiful bright copper eyes like Xanther's.

A stone golem thrust up through the platform in front of me, and a thin copper strand of something like wire floated down from Lady Chandrelle and wrapped around its thick but roughly humanoid neck.

"You will be wearing this thread for the duration of our hearing," Lady Chandrelle informed me in a soft-spoken conversational tone. "If I do this"—she held up a slender hand and pressed her thumb and forefinger together—"any being wearing the thread will be decapitated."

The copper strand had responded instantly to her gesture, but it took several extra seconds for gravity to demonstrate its efficacy. The golem's boulder-like head slid off its neck, no doubt carefully sheared at an angle for just this purpose, and crashed to the floor at my feet.

I leaped backward so it didn't break my toes.

No one else so much as blinked.

But as that damn copper thread floated back into the air and hovered above me, I was abruptly grateful for the walkers' innate stillness.

Had Lady Chandrelle ever forgotten herself and pressed her thumb and forefinger together by accident?

"I should also mention," Lady Chandrelle continued in that same soft-spoken tone, "that should I die while you're wearing the thread, you will certainly die with me. For the thread will react to my demise in the exact same fashion as I just demonstrated."

And then the copper thread—or garrote more accurately—wrapped itself around my neck.

This wasn't a good start.

CHAPTER NINETEEN

The eldest steel-haired walker spoke again. This time he was addressing me.

"Wildcard Nova, against our better judgment, we gave you a chance to prove yourself. And you have proven yourself unworthy of that trust."

He peered down at me like he was inspecting the innards of a slug that'd had the gall to smear his shoe.

So much for Zaltarre's idea of earning points for hiking up the stairs.

"What vested interest do you hold in walkers leaving your world?"

"Um, what?" My mind scrambled to make sense of his words. What the heck was he talking about?

"That is why you drained Lord Brackenfort, is it not? To ensure the decision would go through?"

"What decision?"

The mind mage had come forward to stand level with me but was maintaining enough distance to send a clear message. Now she spoke for the first time. "Her confusion feels genuine."

Lord Brackenfort rubbed his chin thoughtfully. "It's possible she did not know of our secret vote. That was the intention of it being secret after all." His hand dropped to the throne's armrest. "Indeed, only the members of this council should have known about it."

"Oh, *enough*, Lord Brackenfort," said a raven-haired woman in a tone of exasperation. "I understand you're upset to have been so violated in your own home and then to have lost the vote as well, but the decision has been finalized. There is no need to insinuate conspiracy among our own."

Lord Brackenfort waved a hand toward me. "Then let us ask the perpetrator. Why did you do it? Are you so eager to get rid of us that you're prepared to doom your world to do it?"

"No!" Although I had been once. "Please. What are you talking about?"

"*You* are the one here to be questioned," someone hissed.

I bit back my frustration. In this matter I *was* the transgressor. Although no more than Lord Perridor, who was sitting there on his pompous throne, looking down at me with condescension to match the rest of them.

The eldest walker, the one with the heavily jeweled fingers, seemed to be taking point on this interrogation. "If you did not know of the vote as you claim, why did you drain Lord Brackenfort to near death?"

It was a reasonable enough question. Dammit. But one I couldn't answer without revealing Lord Perridor's hand. And if I revealed Perridor's hand, he would no doubt reveal how we'd met and why I'd agreed to do his dirty work. Which meant Theus would be dragged before this council, and attempting to defend his actions with his belief that I was the prophesied one and he'd needed to protect me was not going to go over well with this audience. Which meant he would be executed for treason.

So I scrambled for a lie—I glanced at the mind mage—no, a *half-truth* that I could feed them without ousting anyone else.

"I was paid to do it by one of your kind."

Lord Perridor stiffened, but the reaction was so slight I would never have noticed had I not been watching for it. "Paid?" he repeated distastefully. "Such a human concept. With what?"

Damn he was smooth.

"Protection," I answered.

That was true enough.

Steel-hair steepled his bejeweled fingers. "And who promised you this *protection* for such a despicable act?"

I didn't really *know* the person's identity, did I?

They could've told me anything. True, Theus might've known if they were lying, but *personally*, I couldn't confirm they were who they'd claimed to be any more than I could name the unfamiliar members of the council in front of me.

"I don't know," I said, concentrating on the part of that statement that was true.

The mind mage tilted her hand back and forth in a gesture I took to mean "sort of."

"What did the walker look like?"

Lord Perridor's image flashed in my mind, and I quickly focused on each of the council members in turn so it would seem innocuous if the mind mage had picked up on it.

"You think a walker with political machinations in mind would be foolish enough to come in their true guise?" I asked them. Never mind of course that this unnamed walker hadn't expected to stumble across us. "I don't know that either."

The mind mage was shaking her head, so I added, "I mean, the walker appeared to be male with dark hair and light skin if that helps, but that's all I can tell you."

There, that was vague enough not to pinpoint Perridor while giving me at least the *impression* I was trying to cooperate.

"What did you need protection for?" Lord Brackenfort asked with genuine curiosity.

Dammit, why did I have to drain the only seemingly decent member of the council? And whatever that implied about Perridor's motives, it wasn't good.

My voice was more bitter than I intended. "If you treated attacks on humankind with the same weight as one of your precious council members, I wouldn't have needed it."

Because that was true. I wouldn't have needed to go to the cache in the first place if they'd treated Ellbereth's attempts on my life more seriously. Sure, it wasn't what I'd bargained with Perridor over, but it was a direct consequence.

Unfortunately, the council seemed unaffected by my accusation.

"If you want us to show any leniency," insisted the imperious old codger leading the proceedings, "then you must cooperate. What form of protection did this person offer?"

I thought hard but came up with no safe answers. "I cannot say."

"How did you meet them?"

"It was a chance meeting. Or so I thought at the time."

"Where?"

"I cannot say that either."

The exasperated raven-haired woman spoke up again. "Enough! The human is uncooperative and recalcitrant even now. Why should we spare her? Even if her story is true and she did this at the behest of a walker, then by neutralizing her, we disarm the conspirator. And if she's lying"—here she shot a suspicious look at the mind mage who winced—"then she should be killed. Either way, we've wasted enough time listening to her half-truths. It is clear that we should never have acquiesced to the prophecy-believers' wishes in this matter, and we have allowed this dangerous foolishness to continue long enough. She is a threat, and she must be executed."

Lady Neryndrith spoke then for the first time. "I disagree."

The other council members reacted with surprise.

"Since when have you been a human sympathizer?" asked a walker with golden hair as fine as spider silk.

"I'm not. Imprison her for all I care. It merely seems an extreme judgment given she hasn't killed anyone herself."

"But she's harmed them," argued the same exasperated woman who apparently wanted to speed up my execution so she could get home for breakfast. "And she's shown her willingness to use her wicked magic against our kind. No. We gave her a chance to prove herself, and she proved herself unfit to hold such power. Regardless of whether she acted as our enemy or was used as an ignorant instrument, she is too dangerous to let live."

There were murmurs of agreement around the dais.

Lord Perridor remained silent. Perhaps this had

been his intention all along. That I die and thus forever protect his secret.

Feeling panicked, I stared directly at him until he returned my gaze. I wanted to unnerve him. To suggest I might break unless they gave me this much.

"If I'm going to die for this, then I want to understand why. What do you mean the walkers are leaving? How? When? Why? Where to?"

Lord Perridor must have interpreted my threat correctly, because he deigned to answer. "For the first time in fifty years, we will be allowing walkers to return home." He said this with obvious satisfaction. "At first our world was too decimated to support more than the population of hollows who couldn't flee with us, but fifty years have passed and enough regeneration has taken place to change that. However, until now, it was forbidden for anyone to return. Because the intention coming to this world was not only to save ourselves and our hollows but also to fulfill the prophecy and claim victory against the Malus. To return home before doing so would be to admit failure, defeat, and no one would agree to surrender their children to the doomed war effort then. Beyond that, it was a matter of pride."

"It is a matter of *responsibility*," Lord Brackenfort corrected, his sad eyes on me. "Which some are willing to shirk. Lord Perridor's only child turns seventeen next year."

That got Lord Perridor to react. "She is my only

child because my wife was already snatched from me! I will not lose her too. For 150 years we have bound and bled, we have sacrificed our children, our future, our hopes, and for what?" His face had turned dark with anger and conviction. "To pay for an honest mistake made by a single walker? Enough is enough. No more!"

I gaped as the immensity of this vote, this decision, began to sink in.

They were going to leave.

And they were *not* going to take the Malus with them.

"But you knowingly brought the Malus here," I protested. "How can you live with yourselves if you doom an entire world to destruction?"

Another councilwoman spoke up, someone who'd remained silent until now. Her anger was icy compared to Perridor's heat.

"Be silent!" she hissed. "We can live with ourselves because our children will *live*. Do not forget that we have already sentenced thousands of hollows —children who together with their descendants should have comprised a significant portion of our future generations—to your same fate. We have already sacrificed their lives, their futures, and for what? There is nothing noble about dying fruitlessly alongside those already doomed. It is merely wasteful."

The damnedest thing was I could see her point. I

hesitated, and that was enough for her and everyone else to brush me aside.

"I will not debate our decision with a criminal who has clearly acted against the best interests of her own kind for selfish reasons," declared the snooty raven-haired walker.

And again, there were murmurs of assent among the council.

I felt like the sky whale that had landed on me earlier had been joined by a dozen more. It was a wonder the unbearable, crushing weight of it didn't drive me through the dais floor.

No more walker hollows to aid us on the war front.

No more ethereally beautiful cities, and strangely, I felt bereft at that.

No more Firstborn Agreement. Which had been the most earnest desire of my heart up until a few months ago. A dream that I'd worked toward, trained for, and schemed about for most of my life, and yet now it was to be fulfilled, the dream tasted like ashes on my tongue. Be careful what you wish for. Because I knew now what it would cost our world for that wish to be granted. And the cost was far too high.

The walkers were giving up. Going home. Leaving the unstoppable slaughter and destruction of the Malus dumped in our laps.

And *I'd* made it happen.

Could *this* be the end that Lirielle's grandmother

had foreseen? What if the final line about the nightmare being laid to rest was only from the perspective of walkerkind?

They could retreat back to the world that could now support them again, knowing that they'd tried and strived and sacrificed. Knowing that at the very least, the Malus would be contained on earth since none of its inhabitants possessed a world walking ability.

Except I did. And the walker hollows did too. *We* couldn't leave this world, but we could still open a gateway to another. Maybe I could force the walkers into staying, into helping, into finishing what they'd started by threatening to release the Malus back onto their recovering world if they didn't?

No. Because I'd be dead.

That threat would only guarantee it.

How many walkers did we need to hold our world in balance? To provide for the human settlements depending on them? And if we ever did defeat the Malus, how many would we need to coax life back into the decimated continents, to keep the Preservatorium functioning and use it to repopulate the indigenous species?

Too many, I feared.

My mind reached frantically in another direction. How old were the hollows they'd left behind on their home world? That had been fifty years ago, and walker hollows with their shortened lifespans only lived for a hundred. How many were still alive? Perhaps instead of the walkers returning home, we could convince them to stay on our world and send the Malus back to theirs. We could save one of the two planets after all. Why not this one?

But did I want that? The walkers permanently settled on our world never able to return to their own? Judging from what I'd seen here today, I didn't think so. Some walkers were good, great even, but in most minds, humans would always be viewed as inferior.

Not to mention there might not be enough life force there to tempt the Malus into relocating.

And why was I bothering to think any of this through at all? The decision had been made, and no one in this circle was going to listen to me.

I was just here to die.

I struggled to rise above my miasma of despair. The realization that *I* had done this.

How would the walker hollows feel, knowing they'd been given up on and left behind? And while not everyone believed in the prophecy, it was clear that many more on the frontline had clung to the hope of a foreseen victory than those who lived safe and tucked away in this city.

For some time a subset of people had believed that *I* was that firstborn human witch, and Bryn had told me that the whispers had risen to new levels after I'd saved Fletcher. *Wait for the reversal of life and death,* the prophecy said, and I held the power of both in my wildcard gift.

Which meant those believers on the frontline would lose the support of their own kind and the supposed prophesied firstborn in a single blow.

I shook my head, the movement making me realize I'd completely forgotten about that copper thread around my neck. "But if you know the vote was tampered with, then you must recast it!"

Lord Perridor had set me up to drain Lord Brackenfort the night of the secret vote, presumably because Brackenfort might have been able to swing the decision the other way. But the council knew that. Not who had held my strings, but *why* Brackenfort had been attacked. So surely—

"We did," the old steel-haired walker said.

Selfishly I thought for a moment that I was saved —at least from the burden that this disaster was my responsibility. Perhaps even that they'd reversed or were considering reversing the decision. But then he went on.

"After the Malus's unprecedented rampage yesterday—a rampage triggered by you, who many have been heralding as the prophesied firstborn— several more members of this council have been persuaded the cause is lost."

Behind me, Lord General Zaltarre cleared his throat. "If I may... Nova's magic is demonstrably not the same as the Malus's as we first believed. And she has been cooperative on the war front, following orders and working well with her unit. Within two short days of her arrival, she single-handedly made the Malus feel threatened for the first time in 150 years. *That* is why it rampaged yesterday. What she did to Lord Brackenfort is extremely regrettable"—I could feel the weight of his gaze on my back—"but she did not take his life. You may be leaving, but me and mine will remain. Leave us this small chance of hope."

I found myself holding my breath. In shock that he would stand up for me after what I'd done, and in hope that it might actually work…

The steel-haired walker leading the proceedings asked, "Have you discovered any potential method by which she might defeat the Malus?"

"Not yet."

He waved one glittering hand in dismissal. "Then there is no reason to spare her." My hope crashed to the floor like the golem's head. "I declare this hearing—"

Lady Neryndrith interrupted. "Wait! She cannot be executed. Almost everyone in this court owes me a favor, and I'm calling on it now. That little bitch bonded with my daughter against her will, so if you kill her, Ellbereth dies too."

"She what?"

"How dare you keep this from us?"

Steel-hair recovered from his evident shock and sputtered, "This is a *major* security risk. That must mean she knows about the Cache of the Last Stand. She could massacre us all with that sort of power!"

Lady Neryndrith held her chin high in stubborn weathering of their complaints.

"All the more damning reason to kill her," declared the soft-spoken walker who controlled my copper garrote. "I'm sorry, Lady Neryndrith. But your daughter will be far from the first casualty of this war."

Ellbereth's mother flinched. "So *you* can so easily say now the vote has gone in your favor. Now that your own children will be spared. Perhaps I will rescind my vote and—"

"The matter has already been settled," snapped Lord Perridor.

Zaltarre interjected again. "I believe Nova's fate is a matter that should be decided by those who will be remaining behind. If nothing else, she has proven she has the capacity to heal those no one else can. That alone is invaluable to us on the war front. The one you are so easily walking away from."

His fury was tightly leashed but audible all the same.

"Yes, you lot should have no further import in council decisions since you're shirking your duty and honor and leaving," someone else snapped.

"We aren't preventing *you* from staying!" the raven-haired woman retorted. "Get over yourself and stop trying to control everyone with your warped sense of duty."

As the argument escalated, I began to wonder a little facetiously if it might be a good thing they were leaving after all. The mind mage had sidled out of sight, and I wished I could do the same.

Lady Chandrelle's soft voice somehow rose above the others. "I fear we are straying from the subject of this hearing, my lords and ladies."

Zaltarre strode forward into the center of the dais, and the full force of his authority was not diminished by the semicircle of raised thrones and their esteemed occupants. "Lady Chandrelle is right. This is a poor display of decorum and duty both. Let us get to the heart of the matter. What is it that you are afraid Nova will do should you let her live?"

Steel-hair sniffed, displeased at having lost his leading role in the meeting. "Her successful attack on Lord Brackenfort and forced binding of Lord Neryndrith's daughter illustrates the risks clearly. She's too dangerous, too powerful, and she cannot be controlled."

"Ah, but there is a way to control her," Zaltarre countered. "She has handed it to us."

The raven-haired walker sounded exasperated again. "What do you mean? Speak plainly."

"As Lady Neryndrith has pointed out, if we kill Nova, Ellbereth will die," Zaltarre explained calmly. "But the reverse is also true. I propose Ellbereth is removed to safekeeping in this city and kept under guard. She can live in luxury, surrounded by her family and friends. And should Nova ever get out of control or go on some power-crazed murderous rampage as you so fear, we can kill her without needing to get anywhere near her. You won't even have to leave the city. Ellbereth can be our safeguard."

Lady Neryndrith did not look pleased with Zaltarre's proposed solution. But she had backed herself into a corner by withholding the secret of what I'd done to her daughter. She'd lost the other council member's favor, her leverage over them, and so she held her tongue in grudging acceptance.

The others looked thoughtful too.

Lord Brackenfort spoke first. "I, as the victim of this crime and a member of this council, find that solution agreeable."

Steel-hair was still frowning. Probably upset he didn't have an excuse to squash the annoying slug after all. But after a moment of consideration, he threw up his hands. "Fine. Who cares? We're leaving anyway."

Lord Perridor, Lady Chandrelle, and the vocal raven-haired walker all shrugged or murmured their assent, and the rest of the council followed suit.

"As for you, Lady Neryndrith," steel-hair added, "we will discuss your failure to act in the council's best interest at a later date." His gaze turned without favor to Zaltarre.

"Lord General, you are free to take your pet with you. Do try to keep her under control this time."

Jaw tight, Zaltarre closed the distance between us

and unwound the copper thread from my neck. "Come along, Armsman Nova."

I should've felt relief. My life was spared. But all I could see as Zaltarre led me away was Lord Perridor's self-satisfied smile…

CHAPTER TWENTY

"I don't need to know the details of why you did it," Zaltarre told me as we translocated back to the war front through the usual series of gateways.

"From Valesk's reports, you have shown yourself to be a valuable and disciplined member of your unit who readily puts herself in harm's way for the welfare of others. So yes, you screwed up big time. But I still believe you might be the answer we need."

"But I've only made everything worse. The Malus is out of control, and the walkers are leaving."

I couldn't remember the last time I'd felt so small.

"Yes," Zaltarre acknowledged. "So take what you've learned from those failures—because you've uncovered more new information about the Malus in two days than we have in decades—and take that guilt you're feeling and *use* it. Use it as motivation to try again. To keep trying until you make things better. Because I believe you can."

I didn't know how to answer.

When my silence stretched too long, the lord general spoke again.

"It is true that you were the catalyst for both the Malus's rampage and the council vote going through. But don't forget you were acting under my orders with the Malus. Nor can you take responsibility for the actions of over half an entire race. You haven't forced anyone to leave.

"Yes, Lord Brackenfort was doing an excellent job of convincing some to stick to their principles and responsibilities, but this decision was inevitable. If not this year, then maybe the next or the one after that."

He exhaled heavily, and for just a moment, the lord general's aura of authority and intensity faltered, and I caught a glimpse of the man without those bastions to hold him up.

His iron strength remained but had been worn down to a bone-deep weariness. For over thirty years he'd pitted his soldiers against an unstoppable foe, ordering them to risk their lives again and again and losing ground day in and day out.

How much did it cost him to be a rock standing against the relentless pounding waves of despair and defeat?

He glanced at me, and his wavering aura steadied. "The contingent of walkers wanting to pull out of this fight and return to their own world has been growing rapidly in recent years. Of course, some still believe they have a responsibility to fix what they started. That viewpoint has held true for the majority for nearly one and a half centuries. But the majority has shifted.

"Newer generations don't feel responsible since it wasn't their doing to either unleash the Malus or bring it to your world. They question why they should pay —and pay in vain—for their ancestors' sins. And older generations are largely burned out. The war has defined their entire lives, and they have only sorrow and death to show for it. They've given up hope, and they're scared for their children and grandchildren."

I could almost understand that, and I had no doubt Zaltarre could too. But neither of us wanted to.

"What effect is their leaving going to have?" I asked.

"Nothing good. It depends how many go. Rations. Shortages. No new recruits. Limitations on the Preservatorium and protections around the human settlements. And if too many leave, I expect we'll see extreme weather and an increase in natural disasters as the balance of the world is pushed closer to the point of failure."

My stomach lurched in a queasiness that had nothing to do with our journey through the final gateway.

Zaltarre's intensity amplified upon returning to the need that drove him. "I must call an assembly so my people aren't blindsided by the news." He glanced at me again. "You'd best stay close until Ellbereth is on her way to the city."

It didn't take long for everyone to gather on a barren plain to hear Zaltarre's address. Anyone not on duty had been roused from their beds shortly after I had for the evacuation, and they'd only just been given the all clear to return.

The Malus, thwarted by the lack of soldiers to murder in their sleep, had now withdrawn and was continuing its regular advance into unconsumed territory. Thank goodness for one piece of good news.

Not everyone was here of course. Those who could not be spared from duty or were still badly injured would have to make do with hearing Zaltarre speak through their squeakers. But even so, it was the first time I'd seen most of the army assembled in one place.

There were thousands and thousands of us. Ten? Twelve? And yet so few compared to the immensity of the enemy we faced. To be all that stood between the world and its complete destruction.

I couldn't help but note the disparity between Zaltarre and his troops gathering on the bare dirt without infrastructure or ceremony, and the council members in their splendid, formidable court.

Zaltarre climbed the ruins of an old farm building so that everyone could see him and magnified his voice.

"I come directly from the council with grave

news," he began. "But you, more than anyone, have a right to hear it, and I don't want you to be ambushed by rumors and misinformation over the coming days. Some of you might have heard whispers of this already. The council has voted to lift the ban on walkers returning to our home world."

I couldn't see everyone's faces, but I could see enough of them to read the general reactions to the news.

Shock. Anger. Despair.

To the walkers, this wasn't just their source of provisions walking away. This was their families, their loved ones, their siblings who had escaped the life sentence of becoming a hollow thanks to their own sacrifice.

This was abandonment.

And each intake of breath, every brow that creased and jaw that tightened, every pair of bright, beautiful eyes that shimmered with unshed tears, piled fresh guilt upon me.

Use it, Zaltarre had advised me. Channel it. Do better.

Maybe I could fix this. Maybe I was the *only* one who could fix this—or at least make it sort of okay.

But *how*?

The humans were slower to react. Confusion at first. Like me, most probably hadn't even known of the ban nor the possibility of it changing. And then, watching their teammates, uneasy certainty that this

166

was bad news, even though they didn't fully comprehend why.

Use it, I reminded myself.

Zaltarre went on explaining the details of the decision. He did not, mercifully, explain my part in it. But that didn't stop me from condemning myself.

Morale was plummeting faster than a dropped rock. The message this council decision sent to those at the war front was clear.

We've given up. The cause is lost. You and your sacrifices don't matter.

The lord general made an attempt to rally his troops.

"Take heart. The vote was close, which means many still believe in our cause and will remain to support us in it." He paused, then shouted, "And we are *far* from defeated!"

The strength of his conviction had even me almost believing it.

His gaze swept the assembled crowd, appearing to touch on each individual. In doing so, he drew them from their reflective shock and horror back to the man they served and respected.

"I am confident that this is the best damn fighting force in recent history. You have stayed strong in the face of overwhelming odds, stayed diligent in the face of too many years. And every day you rise from your bed and put on your armor to do your duty, you overcome a perfect storm of hardship, delayed hope, and seeming impossibility that would make lesser beings crumble. You have sacrificed your lives, your years, and your futures to protect this world. And it is a privilege and an honor to lead you."

A cheer spread through the assembled soldiers, slowly and first, and then rising and swelling to a pitch so loud it reverberated through my body.

Zaltarre waited for it to die down before declaring, "Whatever tomorrow holds, we will face it together." He paused before adding, "*I'm* sure as hell not going anywhere."

And that was how the lord general delivered the most devastating news his forces had ever faced to a round of chuckles and cheering.

CHAPTER TWENTY-ONE

My respect for Zaltarre only rose after witnessing him handle his troops. Me included. He could've rightfully ground me under his heel for what I'd done and then heaped burning coals of public condemnation over my head, but where would that have left me? Bruised and quagmired in guilt and shame.

Instead, he'd lifted me up, made me feel understood and empowered—if not entirely pardoned—and told me he'd believed in me. Which made me want to do my utmost to prove him right.

If I hadn't already been wholly committed to finding a way to defeat the Malus, his treatment of me would've ensured it.

As the gathering broke up, he sent one of his aides to bring Ellbereth to him. And the pair of us awkwardly followed him back to command headquarters.

Well, *I* felt awkward. Ellbereth might've felt the same, but she looked as she usually did, graceful, calm, and unflustered. Of course that didn't stop her from shooting me venomous glances that no one else would catch.

Zaltarre gestured for me to take refreshments at a small table outside while he spoke with her in his office.

The fruit juice waiting for me was probably sweet and flavorsome, but it tasted like sand as I considered whether it would be available as more and more walkers left our world.

Even if enough walkers initially stayed behind to perform the most necessary functions, how many of them would later be lured away by that ever-present temptation? The knowledge of their friends and family members returning home to a Malus-free existence while things grew worse and worse here. How long would it take for their resolve to crumble?

Too many, too quickly, I feared. A great deal too many.

I spared little thought for Ellbereth's fate. Whether she'd be pleased to return to a life of luxury or annoyed that the council had deemed her greatest value was to act as my very own kill switch.

I had bigger problems.

How the heck could I hope to stop the Malus? Ripping away its life force, the one ability given to me by my wildcard magic, was unfeasible. The Malus would surge and rampage and slaughter and regenerate faster than I could rip chunks from it and recover from the withdrawals. Nor could I hope to overpower and drain the immensity of its worlds-containing energy in a single encounter.

Which left me with what? A cranky old sword and Ellbereth's walker magic that I wasn't supposed to use? The same power possessed by thousands of walker hollows that had failed to do more than slow the enemy in all these years?

I rubbed my face and took another sip of sand juice.

Ellbereth reemerged from the headquarters building with one of Zaltarre's aides as an escort. Her face was tight and unreadable as she strode over to me.

"So... our secret's out then."

She sounded amused, but I didn't think she was.

"Whatever you do while you're running around pretending to be the prophesied one, *try* not to be a martyr about it." She flicked her hair over her shoulder. "If it's all the same to you, I'd prefer to enjoy my remaining years rather than die without warning in my sleep."

The aide cleared his throat behind her, and Ellbereth turned and walked away. I didn't bother to watch. I already knew where she was going.

I supposed if there was a bright side to this whole crap storm of disaster, there was a good chance that was the last time I'd ever need to see her.

CHAPTER TWENTY-TWO

Bryn, Ameline, Theus, and Lirielle pounced on me as soon as Zaltarre allowed me to return to my own base.

The living greenery that had modified our living quarters into a kind of oasis was dead. Leached of color and already beginning to disintegrate to dust. But everything else was untouched.

"Are you okay?" Ameline asked.

"What the hell happened?" demanded Bryn. "For the love of all that's bright and flammable, tell us everything. We've been dying here."

"Actually," Ameline interjected, "the other Blob Blast players have been the ones suffering under Bryn's agitation. It turns out the game is portable."

Theus only stared at me with an intensity that flustered me in an entirely different way than the walker council had.

"You're safe," I told him.

His jaw tightened. "It wasn't my own welfare I was concerned for."

I rolled my eyes. "Well *somebody's* got to care about yours. But I'm safe too." Mostly.

He relaxed a fraction. But only a fraction. As if he'd heard my unspoken addendum.

"I kept him where he would be safe," Lirielle assured me.

"Literally," Theus ground out. "She forced me to obey Zaltarre's orders not to follow by magically tying me to a tree."

Lirielle nodded happy confirmation, oblivious to Theus's outrage. And I smiled at her in gratitude.

Which did not help Theus's outrage.

Bryn pointed a finger at them. "I was *wondering* where Theus had gotten to, and I want to hear more about that, but first, Nova." She turned back to me. "Start at the beginning. Like how was it you ended up collapsed over one of the two walkers sent to arrest you and the other nowhere in sight? Did the Malus drain you somehow? Zaltarre whisked you off before we knew anything."

"No. Not exactly. When Vaegon, the walker the Malus killed, collapsed, I could see his life force inside the Malus's so clear and perfect it was as if he was still alive. I thought maybe I could save him somehow, like if I could just feed him some extra energy he might be able to step back into his body."

Bryn slapped her palm to her forehead. "Of course

173

you risked your life trying to save the guy arresting you."

"What happened?" Lirielle asked, suddenly intent.

"I could *feel* what he felt, the same way I did with Fletcher, except he was conscious, so there was more. He was worried for his partner. Could sense the Malus he was now part of reaching out to kill him too. And we could both see he wasn't going to get through the gateway in time. Then Vaegon sort of *pushed* against the Malus somehow, or maybe exerted his will over the tiny section of the Malus he was part of. I'm not sure. But the Malus drew back, just for a second, and his friend made it through."

Ameline was shaking her head. "You mean they're still alive in there? Conscious of what they're part of, but helpless?"

"Not for long, I don't think. It was sort of fraying him at the edges before I gave him extra strength. Like it would only take hours or days before most of you was lost, amalgamated into the Malus..." I trailed off, struck by a fresh realization.

Vaegon had *moved* a tiny piece of the intangible Malus.

"So what happened then?" Bryn prompted.

"Well," I said slowly, my mind focused elsewhere, "Theus disconnected us and then Lord General Zaltarre took me to the Court of Hearing..." I trailed off a second time.

174

Bryn bounced impatiently. But I barely registered the fact.

Because I'd just come up with an idea of how to bring down the worlds-destroying enemy that had gone undefeated for 150 years.

Until this week.

CHAPTER TWENTY-THREE

Under Lord General Zaltarre's oversight, we spent the next few days doing everything we could to check the plan's feasibility. And the more we learned, the more we were convinced that it might just well work.

But we kept the details confined to the Reaper unit and a few of Zaltarre's trusted aides for now, not wanting to raise false hopes.

Meanwhile, news was out about the repeal of the interworld travel ban, and the walkers were departing in droves. Hollows' peers, mentors, allies, parents, siblings, cousins, and friends were abandoning them to their fates. And each departure robbed those walker hollows left behind of not just their loved ones and material support, but of the very significance of their great sacrifice.

To become hollows, they'd given up half their lifespans and the ability to walk between worlds—an ability that defined their species and clawed at their hearts with an innate, powerful desire that would be forever unattainable to them. And now the prestige, honor, and respect that sacrifice was supposed to have earned them, as well as the purpose and significance for which they'd given up so much, was rendered a little more, well... hollow.

In addition to the ongoing erosion of hope, morale, and purpose, preemptive provisioning was already being put into effect to prepare for future shortages.

If our plan had any hope of working, the sooner we actioned it, the better.

But stars, it was risky. How many lives would it cost? How many volunteers would we ask to sacrifice even more than the walker hollows already had? To sacrifice everything.

Hundreds? Thousands?

We didn't really know, though Zaltarre had made an attempt to calculate it. Too many, wherever the answer lay. And our final figure would likely be determined by the number of walkers willing rather than any calculation.

It was an impossible request to make: to ask individuals to lay down their lives for an unproven theory. Because whether we succeeded or failed, their deaths would be guaranteed.

We were not only asking them to die, but to potentially die for nothing.

Yet we couldn't test the plan on a smaller scale first. The Malus learned from its mistakes, and this strategy leaned heavily on the element of surprise.

We would have one shot and one shot only.

The steep cost and risk of failure made me acutely uncomfortable. And my friends made it plain they were unhappy about the likelihood of my own death. But I couldn't let any of that stop me when the entire world was at stake. Better to die trying than succumb to fear and despair.

Besides, what alternative was there other than to literally watch the world die?

With so many walkers leaving, the Malus left unstopped, and the earth's balance edging closer to catastrophic failure, the conditions for those stuck here would worsen and worsen. Right up until the end that would come far too soon.

So I kept reminding myself.

Lord General Zaltarre had assured us that we couldn't expect to defeat an enemy as vast and powerful as the Malus without sacrifice. But even he'd sagged under the weight of those certain deaths. The sheer *number* of them.

He hadn't let it stop him either. Which was why he'd gone to the walker council to present our plan and appeal for their support. And why our entire Reaper unit was currently fidgeting in Zaltarre's office, waiting for him to return.

He was late.

Silvyr was juggling spheres of light again. The feat was less impressive than it looked given gravity had nothing to do with it.

Dax, Orlandrus, and Bryn were threatening to get a game of Blob Blast going in the lord general's office if he didn't come back soon. Ameline was feeding Griff tidbits and speaking quietly with Fletcher. Lirielle was coaxing a tender green vine to grow from a pot in the corner and making polite introductions between it and the ghost of its predecessor. And Theus, Helena, Xanther, Valesk, and I were all stiff and silent and staring at the door.

We needed the council's support to find the volunteers, and without volunteers, the plan was over before it started.

Then the door swung open, and there was Lord General Zaltarre. Two hours later than we'd expected him.

He had a good game face, but I'd observed him at close quarters over the past several days, and one look at the rigidity of his shoulders was enough.

The news was bad.

"The council has outright refused to work with us on this," he reported tersely. "They told me to 'find another way.' As if we have other options to choose from." He glanced almost peevishly at me. "Half the imbeciles are convinced that this whole thing is a scheme Nova has concocted to inflict revenge upon walkerkind, and one even suggested she was working in tandem with the Malus."

Bryn bristled, but I laid a hand on hers to stop her leaping to my defense. No one in this room thought those things.

But my stomach revolted all the same. And abruptly, I found it hard to breathe.

This was my fault.

The end of the world would be my fault.

Rationally I knew I couldn't shoulder that blame alone, but I had never expected my deal with Lord Perridor would have such far-reaching consequences. Could never have anticipated draining one single walker to mere unconsciousness might stack council opinion so far against me that they would shut down the one chance we had of defeating the Malus. That they would see only conspiracy when presented with hope.

But just because I hadn't seen it coming didn't make it any less a result of my actions. Theus had tried to warn me.

Yet what else could I have done? Kill Lord Perridor when he'd walked in and found us?

Yes, I thought grimly, maybe that would've been better.

Too late now.

Silvyr broke the bleak silence. "I think I speak for all of us when I say that sucks more than a kraken's suck hole."

Zaltarre's lips twitched in a humorless smile. "That's about the sum of it. After wasting my time with the council, I made some inquiries among my old peers. The misery of it is, four days ago I might have been able to convince some of them to do it. To sacrifice themselves. Because four days ago their fates were intertwined with ours, and the end of the world was looming near. But now that they have the option, the temptation, the freedom, and the hope of returning to our home world, no one was willing to even entertain the idea of making that sacrifice."

I swallowed past my constricted throat. Because heaven help me if that wasn't my fault too.

Zaltarre rubbed a hand over his face, the lines around his eyes and mouth deeper than they'd been a few hours prior.

"I'll keep thinking. We'll all keep thinking. But as it stands, the plan is called off indefinitely."

CHAPTER TWENTY-FOUR

I fell into a despair so deep I wasn't sure I would ever get out again.

My friends tried to help.

"It's not your fault."

"We'll work something out."

"No one could have seen this coming."

And, "Get the hell out of bed before I light it on fire."

That sort of thing.

Bryn *did* light my bed on fire.

It didn't help.

How could anything help when I felt like I'd single-handedly doomed our world?

Rationally I knew better. Knew too that such a burden wouldn't be mine if I hadn't also been supposed to single-handedly save it.

But part of me had believed I might.

Not anymore.

CHAPTER TWENTY-FIVE

The day it happened started like every other recent day. In a shroud of misery.

Bryn forced me out of bed. Ameline gently prodded me into eating something at breakfast. Griff ate most of what I didn't (he was getting a little tubby). And Gus told me to stop moping listlessly about like bloated carrion, or he'd call down a pack of scavengers to finish me off just so he didn't have to watch any longer.

I ran through the training and fitness regime Valesk insisted we do every day before duty. But I performed sluggishly, my heart no longer in it.

I was executing a sloppy set of defensive exercises when a voice dripping with condescension shouted, "I've seen withered earthworms pull off that maneuver with more pizzazz than that! Shape up, Armsman, or I'll reward your slovenly efforts with a ten-mile run."

I spun, oddly pleased to see Professor Cricklewood scowling in my direction. But that moment of gladness died as I recalled how even the cranky old teacher had placed his hope in me. He along with the many others who'd done the same.

Hope that would go unanswered.

Cricklewood had once told me that the only reason he'd bothered to outlive his partner—a hollow who'd died on the frontline of their home world—for a hundred bleak and bitter years was because he wanted to see this war ended before he died.

Somehow I didn't think this was the end he'd had in mind. With earth destroyed and the walkers wiping their hands of the mess, leaving more hollows to die in vain.

Why hadn't Cricklewood gone home? The Firstborn Agreement had been abolished, although the human settlements didn't know it yet, and the academies had been shut down days ago. I'd been wondering if Millicent was lonely.

The professor stabbed his staff into the barren dirt as if he knew how far my attention had wandered. "Rumor has it that you need some foolish old coots to sacrifice themselves."

He paused, his blue eyes raking over me in evident assessment. "Well, I can get them for you."

CHAPTER TWENTY-SIX

Just like that, the plan was back on.

Zaltarre seemed to grow more vibrant with the news that Cricklewood had talked 372 elderly walkers into volunteering for the task.

Elderly walkers who, like Cricklewood, were entering their final years. Who had lived through the best part of two centuries, witnessed the entirety of the 150 years of fighting, and could personally remember the time before the Malus had turned their people's existence on its head.

These elderly walkers were prepared to give up their lives now for a chance to end it. A chance to restore the balance. A chance, in part, to redeem walkerkind in the eyes of humanity and pave the way for a brighter future.

Three hundred and seventy-three (for Cricklewood

himself was among the volunteers) was a lot less than the thousand Zaltarre had calculated we might need. But it was as good a shot as we were going to get.

And so every base was a bustle of activity as the army scrambled to make ready.

Which made it absurd that Zaltarre had given everyone on the incursion team the day off. But we had the most important part to play tomorrow, and he wanted us rested and fresh.

The fact we were also most likely to die was left unsaid.

Ameline surprised me by disappearing early in the morning before I even woke. Fletcher had apparently gone with her. They'd been spending more and more time together since the day he'd come so close to dying. At first I'd assumed it was because Ameline was helping with his recovery the way she did with mine in her warm and patient way. But I was starting to wonder if there was something more… Something I'd been too deep in my own guilt and despair to notice.

If there was—if dear, ever-charming Ameline had snuck past Fletcher's defenses after I had failed and was teaching him how to embrace life and love again —I was only too happy to be left at a loose end for the day.

Bryn talked me into playing a game of Blob Blast, which I promptly and definitively lost.

I retreated to the shower to scrape off all the black

gunk clinging to my hair and skin, and vowed never to play against her again. But when I emerged from the bathroom, she ambushed me with an agenda of an entirely different nature.

"So… you and Theus," she began. "You two have been making goo-goo eyes at each other for months now."

"We have not—"

"You're about as subtle as a brick to the face."

It's true, Gus chimed in uninvited (since the habit of carrying him everywhere with me had been hard to break). *Watching you two blunder around has been excruciating to watch. It's fortunate I don't possess eyeballs, or I might have surrendered to the urge to claw them out.*

I sputtered, "I don't know what you're—"

Bryn cut me off. "Orlandrus told me walkers and humans are sexually compatible."

My eyes got so wide I was worried they might pop out of their sockets—even without the aid of Gus's hypothetical clawing. "That is *not* what's been holding me back!"

Bryn snickered. "Ah, so you admit you've been holding back. That's a good first step. Now you just need to stop being a rockhead and run into the arms of your hot walker lover already."

Recognizing her goading for what it was, I forced myself to take a few breaths before answering.

"Okay, fine," I admitted. "I've thought about it. But we're here for war, not romance."

She tossed her head. "Why not both?"

"I don't remember sitting through a single warfare strategy lecture where they advised us to split our focus."

"What about the one on keeping up morale?"

I plopped down on my bed and crossed my arms in self-defense. "I tied my morale to a cat and sent it up a tree so it can't get down."

"Ohhh, is that why I had to set your mattress on fire… because you were in such a good mood?"

"I did the cat thing *after* that," I grumbled.

She smirked again but didn't relent. "Be that as it may, think about it. Life is short—we of all people should know that—and you deserve happiness, Nova. If my upbringing taught me anything, it was to grab the good wherever you can get it."

I didn't have a comeback to that, so I said nothing. Bryn hid a lot of wisdom beneath her devil-may-care exterior.

She moved to the door. "Either that or you can come and play another game of Blob Blast with me."

I groaned.

She smirked a final time and left me alone to *think about it*.

I was still thinking about it hours later. Although I had at least moved locations. I was standing on the outskirts of the base again, partly to get away from the bustle of the other units preparing for tomorrow and partly to search for answers in the sky.

Not that I expected to find them.

All trace of the plants that had once softened the base's utilitarian hard lines were gone. A reminder that tomorrow I too might be gone. Or perhaps worse, I might survive only to lose many of the people I loved most.

The bare brown dirt that the greenery had once sprung from served as a reminder of how fleeting and fragile life could be.

Ameline had come home smiling but refused to tell me what she'd been doing all morning, saying only, "You'll see."

Fletcher had been somber, but he'd been smiling more often lately. It was not the same smile that had once lit up entire rooms with its warmth and kindness and optimism, but I was glad to see it and the positive progress it represented.

Did that mean Bryn was right? Certainly Fletcher holding himself at arm's length from everyone after the tragedy of his friend's death had done him no favors.

But I wasn't holding Theus at arm's length. I was just resisting the urge to kiss him.

As if summoned, the man I'd been thinking about all day came up to stand beside me.

"If your mind is going to travel so far today, you really ought to pack a sandwich," he said, handing me the lunch I'd forgotten to eat.

"You're too young to be so sensible," I chided. But I took the sandwich.

He was also too young to die.

Stars. He was *so* young. We were all so young. Theus, Ameline, Bryn, Lirielle. And Fletcher, Silvyr, Dax, and Orlandrus too. Even Helena and the oldest armsmen here might be barely halfway through their years if the world were a kinder place.

I thought about the reasons I'd held back. The fear that I'd hurt Theus more deeply if I allowed us to grow closer. Maybe more deeply than his wounded spirit could bear. Wouldn't it be selfish to kiss him now on the eve of my probable death?

But I wasn't the only one risking my life tomorrow.

Maybe it was more selfish *not* to share how I felt about him. More selfish to never offer him the chance to choose for himself how he'd care to risk his heart.

Then there was that new fear. A deeper, hidden one. The fear that the more good I had in my life, the harder it might be to give it all up in the final confrontation.

And yet what if Theus died tomorrow and I somehow survived? I would forever regret not telling him how I felt.

Or maybe we would both be killed. The risk was imminently real. Why hadn't I considered it before?

What if this was our one and only chance to experience romantic love? To follow our hearts instead of the path prescribed for us by duty?

My life had never been about my own desires. As a firstborn, I'd been groomed for sacrifice, for the survival of my family, my bloodline. And Theus had grown up in an age where world walking, the thing he was created for, the thing he most desired, was forbidden, and then had the possibility of it forever snatched from him by becoming a hollow. Later, at least according to some, we'd become the prophesied ones, destined to save the world from the Malus. (Even if Theus believed his role was merely to keep me alive long enough to pull it off.) It was not a destiny one could turn away from.

So no, our lives had never been about our own desires.

But dammit, I was going to steal this moment for us.

I took Theus's hand. The same one that had passed me the sandwich that I now felt too nervous to eat. The same one I'd shaken on our first day of the academy when he'd stayed behind to help the human kids survive the trial. The same one that had brushed the wet hair from my face after saving me from drowning. The same one that had wrested me back from the Malus. It was warm and callused and larger than my own.

Theus didn't draw away. He might have even sidled closer. Or perhaps he just *felt* closer.

Every part of my body had become hyperaware of him. His lithe, muscled form, several inches taller than me. His unruly chestnut hair stirred by the breeze. The beauty of his clear-cut features, the fathomless green eyes that had always drawn me in, the scattering of freckles across his nose that I knew by heart, and those lips… Heaven help me, he was beautiful.

My heart drummed in my chest like it was urging me onward, and every nerve ending sparked with electricity as if they'd been switched off until now.

I licked my lips.

"Would you…? Do you…?" I tried. Then I gave up on words and kissed him.

He kissed me back.

He tasted like mint and starlight. Which was ridiculous. But damn it was so good I almost moaned.

My feelings for him went far deeper than physical attraction, but there was no denying it existed. The press of his lips on mine made my toes curl and heat blossom in unfamiliar places.

Then he pulled back.

I realized with some embarrassment that one of my hands had made its way up to tangle in his hair.

"Are you sure?" he asked, and his voice was lower and rougher than usual, which eased my embarrassment a smidge. "I thought you still had reservations about walkerkind?"

"I do. But I have none whatsoever about *you*."

He took me at my word—either that or his ever-careful restraint chose that moment to set him free. His lips didn't just kiss me, they claimed me. Gently, attentively, as was Theus's way, but unhesitating and insistent. I felt myself quiver like a musical instrument being tuned to the right chord. To him.

I'd imagined what it might be like to kiss Theus.

My imagination was crap.

I felt like I was falling. Or diving deep, deep down into the well that I'd sometimes thought of him as. But even though Ellbereth's administrations had given me a fear of drowning, I wasn't afraid. Not even a little.

Because he was here with me. And I was floating. Or flying. I didn't know which. But the electric, rushing joy I felt was like that of flying with the stormriders, except on more levels and more solid, substantial somehow. Parts of me I'd been unaware of came alive beneath his touch.

Bryn was right. I should have done this sooner.

And it turned out we didn't need words. We'd done plenty of talking over the past months. Not only with speech but with actions that spoke clearly of how we felt. We'd supported each other, cared for each other in dozens of ways small and great, and put our lives on the line to protect one another on multiple occasions. So now we communicated in a different way entirely. A new, wondrous way.

I could've kissed him forever.

As it was, we only had hours. But we certainly made the most of them.

CHAPTER TWENTY-SEVEN

The next day would have dawned far too soon even if it had not been the one that would decide the fate of the world.

But I couldn't regret what I'd allowed Theus and I to share. Kissing my "hot walker lover" was absolutely a more effective morale booster than attempting to get it stuck up a tree. And somehow I felt both more vulnerable and yet stronger at the same time.

I should have known it would be so. Theus had always lent me strength, never taken it from me. The light in his eyes and the curve of his lips was all I needed to know it was the same for him.

I wished we might see what we could do together, he and I, in a world that would allow us the time and space to learn and live and grow old. But that's what we were fighting for, and I prayed that my friends at least would survive to see it.

Today I would need more than the love of Theus and my friends. I would need the strength of hundreds, maybe thousands. As many as we could get in as short a time as possible.

To that end, the Reaper unit and every armsman with a lick of mind magic or affinity with other species traveled through a series of gateways to one of the remnants of our world still flourishing and abundant with life.

Lord General Zaltarre had mentioned something about preparations and told me not to worry about how I'd get the life energy I would need for today. For once, I'd listened, so I didn't know what I to expect. But it wasn't *this*.

My jaw dropped.

Ameline grinned.

We were standing on a sloping hilltop overlooking a wide green valley. Stretching before us from one side of the valley to the other was the strangest assembly I'd ever seen.

Predator sat beside prey. Embercats beside storm-riders, skyfuries beside full-sized griffins, a pack of huge silver wolves beside a herd of green deerlike creatures so shy I'd never seen one. I counted thirteen black locust birds disguised among the other trees and refraining from eating any of the creatures sheltered beneath their canopies. Half a dozen dragons—who were notorious for refusing to ally themselves with anyone—curled on rocky promontories nearby, their scales glinting. And even Professor Wilverness and her glorious antlers was there in centaur form with a small group of other antlered shapeshifters.

Everyone was packed in so tightly that the greenery of the valley was eclipsed by living flesh.

Ears flicked, tails twitched, nostrils flared, and feathers and fur ruffled in discomfit, but they stayed otherwise motionless in uneasy truce. Thousands of creatures, many of them beings that would have had no hesitation trying to eat me had I wandered past them in the forest, beings I'd so often thought of as *monsters*, were here. Willing to offer me their life energy to stop the enemy that threatened us all.

My throat grew tight.

This was what Ameline and so many others had been about yesterday, spreading the word of our need and cause to all intelligent enough to grasp it. And those beings in turn had spread the word farther and farther into places that no human or walker had trod in many years.

The incredible assembly before me was the result.

The immensity of this honor, this trust, this unprecedented cooperation blew me away. Two weeks ago, I had stared at the wide-open sky, wanting to take comfort in my own insignificance. But with the weight of being the prophesied firstborn on my shoulders, I hadn't found the comfort I'd sought.

Now, however, with so many living, breathing, feeling beings going against instinct and defying the natural order of things to aid me, I began to realize just how small a part I would play in all this. A vital part, yes, but only a tiny fraction of a much, much larger cosmic whole.

It also drove home just how important and yet formidably ambitious was the task we were going to attempt. I knew this was only the beginning of the sacrifices I would witness today.

So dammit, I wasn't going to start crying already.

Wilverness and the other Antellians, along with Ameline and those with mind magic we'd brought with us, walked around with sharp blades or equally sharp magic, nicking the skin of the beings that had come to offer me their strength. I took what was offered, using my wildcard gift to drink from their life force until they had only enough to slink, stalk, slither, hop, flap, or otherwise move away. Then the next wave of beings came forward to stand within reach of my magic.

Energy inundated me, waking every one of my senses to near-painful brilliance. My blood thrummed with it. My nerves sang. And still I drank more. And more. And more.

My head felt like it might explode from the sensory overload. The buzzing under my skin was so intense I kept glancing down, expecting to see it writhing as if a swarm of wasps were seething through my veins. And still I drank more.

I had never taken so much. It hurt. It felt like I'd

entered a new plane of existence. And time slowed to treacle, all the better to enjoy every roaring, buzzing, glorious, painful moment.

Finally the creatures stopped coming.

The vast sum of their life forces was far too much to be contained by one frail human. The power pulsed inside me, alive and wild, like a tiger hurling itself against the confinement of my rib cage, trying to break free.

I sensed intuitively that I would need to restrain myself. That if I moved as fast as I was able with the power I felt rippling inside me, I would snap bones and tear muscles.

Never mind that they would heal quickly enough.

Because I had to save every drop of this power for the true heroes of this day.

The elderly walkers who would surrender themselves to their most hated enemy… and were relying on me to ensure they didn't do so in vain.

CHAPTER TWENTY-EIGHT

Three hundred and seventy-three walkers willing to die. Three hundred and seventy-three. It was so many, too many, and yet I didn't know if it would be enough.

A small crowd of us had assembled to stand witness to their sacrifice, including Lord General Zaltarre, the majority of the army's unit commanders, and the entire Reaper unit. Everyone else was busy making final preparations or grabbing what sleep they could after being on duty all night.

We stood a mere hundred yards from the Malus's edge. It had calmed again in this past week, returning to its slow but inexorable advance. But we did not mistake slowness for safety.

The Ice Raven unit, who'd arrived first, was holding open a huge gateway to the void between worlds. This was to act as a shield of sorts to discourage the Malus from jumping forward and snatching the 373 walkers before they were ready. Those of us safeguarded from the Malus's life-force-ripping power stood at each edge of the void shield in a second futile layer of protection.

Few non-hollows had ever been this close to the Malus and lived.

We would not be changing that today.

The solemn and tragic purpose of the occasion subdued even the power prowling within me. Though the beast lashed its tail and promised retribution for making it wait.

For all the significance that walkerkind ascribed to stature and honor, the elderly volunteers did not stand on ceremony. They had been briefed about the plan in its entirety, they had set their affairs in order, and what they were here to do would gain them no reward that they could ever enjoy.

They were here to end the nightmare. The 150-year ordeal that had defined their lives and would now define their deaths too.

Cricklewood appeared to speak for all of them when he pitched his voice to carry. Not quite the drill-sergeant tone he'd used at the academy to bludgeon kids into shape, but close enough that mine wasn't the only former student's spine that automatically straightened.

"Three generations of walkers and millions upon millions of peoples and creatures have fallen beneath the shadow of this relentless Devourer. I will count it the highest honor if mine is one of the last lives it ever takes."

And then he stepped up to me at one edge of the void shield and chucked me under the chin. "Good luck, Armsman Nova."

Without giving me time to respond, he swept past the void shield and stomped toward the greedy, grasping mists of the enemy.

My heart and throat ached as I watched his familiar figure stride alone and willing to the waiting darkness. The thud of his walking stick sent puffs of lifeless dust into the air, and the trailing end of his long white beard seemed to wave back at us with every step.

The professor that had loomed large and intimi-dating over my class at the academy was utterly dwarfed by the towering, menacing blackness. He seemed to grow smaller and smaller the closer he got. But he kept his head held high and did not waver.

One moment he was stomping proudly and defi-antly forward. The next he was falling.

My supercharged senses—or perhaps it was sheer ordinary horror—made me watch in agonizing slow motion. His walking stick slipped from his fingers, and he crashed to the earth without so much as an arm flung out to soften his landing.

Bereft of the force of his prickly but powerful personality, his crumpled body was just that. A small pile of age-ravaged flesh and the blue fabric he favored.

I shut my eyes, wanting to block out that terrible, pitiful, tragic sight. The tears blurring my vision were insufficient for the task.

After our first meeting at the academy, I could never have anticipated that I would weep for the old miser's passing. But I was weeping all right, my eyes streaming and my nose following suit. I had to wipe my face with my uniform sleeve.

And Cricklewood was only the beginning.

What was I *doing* here? The last thing I wanted was to watch all these people die. These grandparents and mothers and fathers and brothers and sisters. These friends and lovers.

But that was why I had to watch. To honor their sacrifices. And so that no matter what happened today, I would not, could not forget the price they'd paid.

So I made myself study every face, to think about the life they must have led, the wealth of skill and knowledge and stories that would die with them, the immensity of their sacrifice. They were far fewer than the thousands of creatures who had donated their life energy to me, but the walkers were giving up far more.

Some wore their best finery, dripping in soft silks and gems. Some wore their house colors and crests, and others wore somber hues and fashions suitable for the occasion. Some went barefoot, as if wanting to feel the earth under their feet one final time, and one elderly couple wore their pajamas.

Some stepped forward into the lethal mists. Others drew close, and then stood and waited for that darkness to roll over them. Some walked the full hundred yards from the void shield. Some translocated right up to the edge. Some, like Cricklewood, faced their end in solitary strength. Others went in small clusters, gaining comfort in solidarity. Couples who had spent their lifetimes together walked hand in hand into death, holding each other until the end.

No matter what they wore or how they went, they all fell the same way.

I forced myself to watch the sacrifice of every single one of them. To bear witness as they gathered their courage and stepped forward past the protection of the void shield. Saw them take in the sight of their fellows already piled upon the scorched earth. Watched as their bodies, bowed by almost two centuries, stiffened in resolve, their wrinkled mouths pinched in grim lines, tears streaming down their lined cheeks, but chins lifted high. And I forced myself to watch as they stepped bravely into the Malus's reach and crumpled.

Never to rise again.

There would be no need to bury their bodies. They would be reduced to dust within a day or two, as irretrievably lost as the souls and minds and hearts that had once filled them.

My second sight sought the forms of their stolen life force within the Malus. Still whole, just for a little while. I watched as those glowing golden walker figures turned and drifted deeper into the enemy that had consumed them. To the rendezvous point. To the core. And heart lodged so tight in my throat it was hard to breathe, I prayed they would remember themselves long enough to do what was needed.

Those minutes—for in real time, that was all it took for a generation of world walkers to die—were the longest and most horrific of my life.

But they forged my backbone into steel for what was ahead. Fortified and burdened me with the excruciating awareness of how much had already been laid down for this plan.

And for how it must—at any cost—succeed.

The last walker fell, sprawling to the blackened earth in an ungainly heap, limbs askew. Then it was time to go.

CHAPTER TWENTY-NINE

It was our turn to enter the darkness.

I looked around at my friends, soaking in the details of each of their faces as they prepared for the end of the world—or the saving of it.

Ameline was pale and grim after saying goodbye to Griff. But I'd seen her slam a dagger into a shadow stalker's skull, wearing that same countenance. Fletcher's expression mirrored hers. Bryn looked a lot like she had just before she'd thrashed me at Blob Blast. Lirielle was tranquil and focused, ready to use her blades. And Theus bore the weight of the world on his shoulders, sharing that burden with me as he'd promised, but I read only determination in his deep green gaze.

My heart ached with love for them, and I wanted to offer some sort of final words. Offer them my thanks for the way they had enriched me, saved me, transformed me. I wanted to articulate how much they meant to me and how freaking wonderful they were. How much poorer my life and the world would be if they weren't part of it.

But my throat was too constricted, and my mind already too numb with grief and horror. So I pressed their hands between mine and sensed, with a sudden flash of insight, that they understood, that they already knew. And my grieving heart felt a little stronger because of it.

Then our unit commander spoke. "All right, Reapers. One minute to go. Let's kick some black blobby butt." And her uncharacteristic informality surprised a snicker out of us.

My pulse quickened.

Our first objective was to get to the rendezvous location. And in this at least, we would be using as much brute force as was practical.

Because the power simmering inside me *had* to be reserved for the very end.

So the Reapers and twenty-four other units that had been handpicked for the final, crucial conflict were crammed into the middle of two hundred additional units. And those additional units would attempt to shield us with their magic, weapons, and lives until we'd punched through to the Malus's core.

It would've been a great deal easier to get to our destination if gateway magic worked reliably within the Malus. But there was something about the enemy's power that interfered. Medium and long-distance translocation could fail altogether, killing everyone passing through, and even short-distance gateways were disorienting. It was one of the reasons few walkers sucked into the Malus by its vortex magic ever came out again. It was also why translocation inside the Malus was prohibited unless you faced a more lethal threat. Why units rushing to offer backup still gatewayed *around* the darkness rather than through.

But time was of the essence, and short-distance translocation was still much faster than walking hundreds of miles. So we would be making use of them today.

The atmosphere among the nearly three thousand armsmen was charged, almost jittery with nervous energy. But every one of the units handpicked by Zaltarre were seasoned veterans (except for me, Ameline, Bryn, Theus, and Lirielle) and knew their specific roles in this operation. Knew how to channel that nervous energy into tightly controlled action.

Then Zaltarre issued the order into every one of our squeakers, and it was go time.

We surged forward, pouring through the first gateway like a bursting dam of flesh and weapons and armor.

The experience of running among nearly three thousand armsmen was part exhilarating and part claustrophobic. The thunderous drumming of our boots against the earth made my heart beat faster and built a momentum of its own that carried me along with it.

But we were used to working in small, agile groups, and while we'd been directed to keep enough distance between each other that we could draw our weapons and use our shield nets as necessary, we were not practiced at it.

Our pace was inconstant and painfully slow to my supercharged limbs and senses. It was difficult to focus only on Valesk's sturdy back in front of me and convince myself over and over that my sole duties were to stay alive and maintain the proper spacing. To rely on those around me to protect themselves and my unit.

Yet though we were unpracticed, we *were* disciplined. So like clockwork, the outer units peeled off to engage the Echoes that morphed into being to meet us and the Taken that came charging in. The rest of us rushed onward through the next gateway flung up by those now in the lead.

The units we left behind to fight would begin a careful retreat as soon as the gateway shut behind us.

My job was to run, and let others do the hard work for me.

But holding on to that conviction was challenging. The darkness obscured everyone's vision despite the best efforts of the individuals assigned to pushing it back. The dust kicked up by thousands of booted feet against the bare earth made visibility worse. I knew my whole unit was pressed around me with orders to protect me at all costs—like valuable cargo too precious to be used. And I knew that they in turn had units pressed around them with the same orders. All the teams chosen for the final conflict did. But I couldn't see them properly.

More than that, I couldn't see what was happening on the outer perimeter. But I could hear the screams of the wounded even without the squeaker conveying them to me, and it went against every instinct not to run to their aid.

The first four gateways, as far as I could tell, went near exactly to plan. Again and again we shed our outer units to protect and distract while the rest of us ran straight onward to maintain our forward momentum.

But each gateway we gained, our numbers decreased, and the darkness grew thicker.

That was part of the plan. Smaller numbers meant we were becoming less unwieldy, our time to transition from one gateway to the next quickening. But it also meant we were more vulnerable.

Then the Malus changed the game.

Perhaps it had only now learned our strategy and was adjusting its assault. Or perhaps it had been waiting until we were deeper inside its clutches and fewer in number.

The next gateway we emerged from was darker still, and we were met with a huge force of flying

Echoes that could not be held off by our outer forces. Monstrous hybrids of griffins, manticores, harpies, dragons, giant bats, and dozens of other species dove from the black, black sky.

They were silent even to my augmented hearing but for the hissing of wind around those stone black feathers and wings that should never have given them the power of flight. They rained death upon our ranks.

Our momentum faltered.

The soldiers ahead slowed and swerved, swearing, to protect themselves. Unit commanders shouted to maintain order, and those with shielding magic threw up an invisible ceiling where they could.

But those of us selected for the final confrontation could not stop and fight. That was the whole point of Zaltarre's punching-through strategy. Leave the rest of the army to engage, distract, and retreat while the core force powered relentlessly forward.

Because if we stopped, if we were cornered, if we lost our momentum to help each other, the Malus would win. The Malus's forces might as well be limitless because we could never hope to match them. Which meant our only chance was in diversion, speed, and surprise.

So I did not stop to help. I did not use my vast reservoirs of power to shield everyone nor use my life force to heal the wounded.

Instead, I dodged around the fallen and kept running, using Gus to slash and slice and sweep through the dark Echoes I could reach—to render what little aid I could without slowing or taxing the power I was striving to keep in reserve.

Zaltarre had given me strict orders so that there would be no gray areas, no room left for me to think in this situation. Only to obey.

"You will leave comrades behind to die," he'd told me gravely, "comrades that you might have otherwise saved, and you will do it on my *command*. Because there is no other way. Their blood will be on my hands. And I will grieve for every single one of them. But I will not alter this heavy charge, this duty you must fulfill. Because if you try to save everyone as is your inclination, you will spit on the sacrifices of all those who have poured out their lives for this mission. And you will save a few lives, maybe even a few hundred lives, at the cost of thousands, at the cost of this entire world and all life on it."

So I did not allow myself to think of the screaming or the fallen. I did not allow myself to think at all. Except of Cricklewood and the 372 others who had walked into certain death to give this mission a chance of success, who were waiting for me, relying on me to do my part.

I forced myself to keep running, focusing on Valesk's sturdy back. But though I tried not to think of the screaming or the fallen, I still *felt* them.

So I reached the next gateway, choking on tears and dust and a thick, warm liquid that I feared was someone's blood. The moisture and dirt were turning into mud, screwing with my already limited vision.

The next section we emerged into was even darker, even more silent. Where were the Malus's forces? Where were ours? Based on the little I heard through my squeaker, the units that had made it through were fewer, more ragged than expected. Losing the feeling that had come from safety in numbers.

Fear struck us hard, pummeling at the protections afforded by our training and the work of those with gifts like Ameline's. And unconsciously we huddled closer together, our pace slowing.

Even with my superior sight, I couldn't see the gateway we were aiming for. Only the press of bodies about three deep in any direction. I focused on following the others, on keeping moving.

Then out of the blackness we heard a low hissing wail, and the ground beneath us began to tremble. However many hundreds of us were left had mere seconds to find space in that tightly packed formation —space to dive to the shuddering earth that we could not see and deploy our shield nets.

The strain of the Malus's fear assault combined with the lethal danger of the vortex power was too much for some. They cried out, pushing and tripping and cowering, wasting time getting to the ground.

Too many failed to make it.

I could not bring myself to ask my own unit who was still there. But Valesk did not shy away from the duty, and it was with guilty relief I heard everyone reply.

The roaring stopped, and we removed our shield nets to a hailstorm of debris that was waiting to smash us to pieces. Again, our unit ducked beneath the shields of others and kept running. I heard something heavy and wet smash against the transparent shield and had a sick certainty it was the remains of one of our own comrades. Someone who'd been alive mere moments ago.

I did not stop.

I was weeping when we at last reached the core. Buzzing with the life force I'd failed to use to save the fallen and emotionally wrung out.

Even with mind magic softening the effect, the fear strangled every breath I took.

Oh stars, the fear…

We were down to a mere twenty-five units at best. Since that was only if everyone had made it. And now we who had been protected by the rest of our forces on the journey here would pay in blood for our former escape.

Because for these three hundred armsmen, there would be no retreat.

Every individual who had made it this far would not back down, would not stop fighting until the end, until it was over. One way or the other.

I searched with my second sight and found the golden light of elderly walker after elderly walker

215

drifting amid the blinding core of the Malus's life force. They had come. They had remembered themselves, remembered the purpose of their ultimate sacrifice. So I remembered too and steeled my spine for what was coming.

The prophecy might only mention two of us that were needed, but this was a group effort. Change would not be wrought by a few individuals but by thousands of them working together. Bleeding and striving and dying for change. For a better future.

For *any* future.

And now they were all relying on me to do my part...

CHAPTER THIRTY

"They're here," I reported, trying to keep my voice from revealing just how shaky I was feeling.

The plan was simple enough. The execution less so.

Pour every drop of the life force I'd clung to at such great cost into the elderly walkers who'd sacrificed themselves for this moment. And buoyed by that power, those walkers would attempt to end the Malus once and for all from within.

I sucked in a shuddering breath.

At least everyone in my unit was still alive. At least that.

But for how long?

All around us Echoes were solidifying before our eyes or emerging from the darkness already formed. We had minutes at best before our meager forces would be overwhelmed.

Give me to Theus since you're not going to be capable of using me, Gus demanded.

The request surprised me. *I thought you'd accept no other wielder?*

He sniffed. *I would not normally stoop to being passed about like a common butter knife, but I find this Malus most bothersome.*

I obeyed, passing his hilt to Theus, who was standing close, who would stay close right up until the end. But there was no time for final words, a final kiss, a final anything.

Because the faster I could finish this, the fewer would die.

Valesk, who was field commander of the final confrontation, spoke. "Razorback and Nightwraith units are on standby to open the gateway. Reaper unit, protect Nova with your lives. Go for it, Wildcard."

Trusting my safety to those around me, I closed my eyes and blocked out the sounds of battle. I needed complete and utter focus to do what was needed. To link myself to Cricklewood and the other 372 walkers within the Malus.

Like Vaegon, the walker who'd arrested me, their life force had been captured and added to the Malus's never-ending reservoir. But also like Vaegon, they had not yet been fully amalgamated, had not yet completely forgotten themselves. I could see their golden figures clearly, still distinct amid the glaring brightness.

All the questions I was trying not to ask flitted through my brain.

How many had already died for this attempt? What if it failed? What if *I* failed? What if it *worked* and Theus failed to shut down my magic and disconnect me in time? And even if everything went perfectly to plan, what would happen after I was drained of the immense power I held?

I shoved the questions aside and concentrated on every single golden glowing walker surrounding us. Something that would have been impossible without my power-enhanced faculties and 360-degree second sight. Then, like when Fletcher was dying, like when I'd tried to save Vaegon, I *pushed* my abundance of life force into them.

For the first two seconds, it was easy.

Then a surge of impressions short-circuited my brain and it wasn't.

Fear not my own flooded me. Fear that came from the connections I'd just forged. For things left undone. For trust misplaced. For the terrifying sensation of having one's self unraveled like a ball of yarn—picked at and prodded and pulled by a thousand unseen hands—getting smaller and smaller until you are no more. Your very existence forgotten. Of feeling yourself fray at the edges as you're taken over by the monster you most loathe, your life force feeding its destructive powers.

I didn't know I'd dropped to my knees until something on the ground cut into them. Every instinct screamed at me to sever the connections, to protect myself, to curl up tight like a freaking armadillo clutching everything precious inside me and wait until the battering stopped. But instead I *gave* of myself, poured myself and my power out like an offering.

It felt wrong, futile, like pouring my only cup of water onto a drought-stricken land, leaving me to die of thirst and achieving a legacy of nothing. But I had not come this far to prove myself a coward. And under the crushing weight of the blood that had already been spilled, I did it anyway.

As I poured, a new surge of sensations hit me. Beneath the fear, for the fear was still there, was purpose. As unwavering as my own. They remembered too. Remembered what we were here for. What was at stake. The reasons they'd given their lives. And they knew that they did not have much more to lose, nor much more to suffer through.

Because they could feel my power pouring into them. Strengthening them. Shoring up their identities, their memories, and that all-important purpose. And the sweetness of oblivion, of absolution, of a triumphant end that would usher in a new era was so close now.

I kept pouring, faster and *more* even though it was beginning to hurt. They needed more. More power. More of me.

Because they were about to attempt to replicate what Vaegon had done.

Each of them would force a piece of the Malus they were now part of to *move*.

Except this time, it would be on a far grander scale.

Because they would have the life energy of thousands of creatures to aid them. Because they were many instead of one. And because they would not merely be shifting the outer fringe of the Malus, but the entirety of its core.

Together, they would shove the core of the Malus —that vital, critical heart of the enemy—through a gateway and into the void. The one thing we knew could destroy it. The one thing the Malus took pains to avoid. The one thing *bigger* than our enemy.

There the Malus would die.

And the walkers would die a second time.

And I would try not to die with them.

That was the plan anyway.

I choked out the pre-agreed signal. "Now."

The Razorback and Nightwraith units opened the void gate. I sensed it not through my own closed eyes but via the dead walkers I was connected to. The gateway was growing larger and larger. And the Malus was recoiling from it.

More. Cricklewood and the other walkers needed more. I sensed it. Or they did. I didn't know which, but I tried to give it to them.

Around me I heard the sounds of fighting, of blades clashing against Echo stone or Taken flesh, of grunts and curses and screams. My friends and comrades dying around me to buy me these seconds.

I gave more. Hell's breath it hurt. At some point over the past minute I had fallen farther. I was on all fours now.

Then sound abruptly cut off. And my entire body was gripped in an iron fist. I couldn't move. I couldn't breathe. I could not so much as twitch.

My own eyes were stuck shut, but I saw what had happened through my connection with the walkers. Saw that where I had been on hands and knees was now a large black boulder formed from the same stuff the Echoes were made of.

I was immobilized in stone.

It felt like drowning all over again. The surge of terror was my own this time. Trapped beneath the ice. Unable to breathe. Except this was worse. I couldn't even move. Couldn't let my chest expand even a fraction. Could not fight at all.

But it didn't matter. The Malus had acted too late. Because my connections could not be severed by stone, and I was so close to empty now. The walkers I had poured my life energy into were glowing bright— so bright—with power. Fleeting power, but that was all they needed.

Dull clinks of blades striking rock reached my ears. Some of my unit trying to free me. To allow me to breathe. To allow Theus to touch me and break the connections at the critical moment.

As one, the walkers flung themselves toward the void, shoving and dragging the core of the Malus with them. I wanted to cry out, *wait!* But I couldn't move, and they could not afford to stop anyway.

Theus wasn't going to reach me in time.

Panic and hope blossomed together in my constricted chest as the first edges of the Malus's core traveled through the gateway and fragmented into the void.

It was working!

But the dimming of my second sight was not Theus's magic at work. The clinks of blade striking stone were louder now but too far away to save me. Because I was being dragged along with the enemy into the void.

And then pain burst across my synapses, and the world—or my awareness of it—ceased.

CHAPTER THIRTY-ONE

My world was dark and hot and cold at the same time. I drowned. Felt the burn of the icy water flooding my lungs. And then I was hot again. And it was dark. But my labored breathing drew in air and not water. And I heard voices, but they were so far away that I couldn't make out any of the words. And then I was drowning again. Or was that sweat that coated my overly sensitive skin? And then I was trapped in the Malus's solid prison, suffocating, captive, unable to draw enough breath to scream. And then I was hurtling into the void with all the walkers who had already died. Gifted themselves to the Malus like the Trojan horse of ancient Greece. And then I was blind. Or was it just darkness? My bones ached. My skin stung as if it had been scoured raw by the power that had possessed me, even the flick of my eyelashes across my cheek was painful. And still my world was dark and hot and cold. Pain and then emptiness took turns clawing and dragging at me. I heard the screams of the wounded and the dying. But they were far away like the voices had been.

Perhaps they were echoes from the past. Perhaps they'd never happened. Or perhaps Theus had not reached me in time and my life force, my awareness, was trapped in the void with the Malus and my memories until my power ran out.

Then I was drowning again as some sort of liquid was forced down my throat, and I thrashed and struggled in fear. And there were more voices.

"She's getting worse. I'm going."

"But—"

"I'm going."

And then there was darkness and fear and drowning, and I could hear only the screams. And then only my labored breaths. And then only silence and darkness and pain.

Then there was nothing at all.

CHAPTER THIRTY-TWO

When my eyes opened, it was like the cracking of an ancient tomb. Stubborn and difficult with a great deal of grit.

My eyelids felt swollen. My eyes stung from the light and whatever hell they'd been engaged in. I tried to lift a hand to at least remove the grit from them, but my arm refused to move.

The tiny slice of the blurry ceiling I could see was unrevealing. But wherever it was, it was *not* the void.

Did that mean we had succeeded then? And that I'd somehow survived?

Except "survived" felt like putting an overly positive spin on things at present.

My mouth felt like something had crawled into it and died and was now halfway through the decomposition process.

I wet my cracked lips, and they joined my eyes in stinging. But that was the sharpest of my pain.

How could that be? My whole body ached in a quiet but all-encompassing sort of way. Like I'd been run over repeatedly by a herd of eight-legged, cloven-hooved goat-spiders. But if this was withdrawal, I'd experienced far worse.

Unless... Was I paralyzed? Was that why my pain was so bearable?

I tried to convince my arm to move again, and this time it twitched. But it felt wrong. I tried my other arm.

Oh. That one worked fine. Well, except for how it felt like it weighed thirty pounds. The rest of my body was working too. Weak, sluggish, but working.

I pushed myself slowly into a sitting position with my good arm and waited for my spinning head to adapt to this new orientation.

The utilitarian room made me think I must be at one of the army bases. And laid out in two beds next to me were Theus and... Ellbereth? What the heck was *she* doing here?

Deciding I didn't give a crap about Ellbereth right now, I focused on Theus. I wanted to rush over to him, but my legs didn't feel capable of holding me.

He was very still. His lips were as dry and cracked as mine felt. His face looked thinner, gaunt, even more sharp-cut than usual. And the circles under his eyes were bruised and sunken. But his chest rose and fell beneath the blanket.

My own breath whooshed out in relief.

Alive. We were both alive.

I noticed without nearly as much feeling that Ellbereth looked equally worse for wear, but she was breathing too. Which made sense since I was apparently still alive.

Did that mean… Could we truly have done it? Defeated the Malus? I couldn't imagine Theus or I making it back to the base otherwise.

But if that was true, where were Ameline and Bryn?

Through every one of my numerous prior withdrawals, Ameline had been there nursing me back to health, her presence a constant I could always rely on. And while Bryn's fire and impatience made her a poor caregiver, she'd rarely left our dorm room until I'd recovered.

For just a moment, I looked into a future without them in it. Color and joy leached away. My heart felt like a cold dead weight in my chest. But before I could fall to pieces, the pair of them burst through the door.

Ameline spotted me sitting up and dropped the glass she was carrying. It shattered over the timber floor, sloshing orange liquid everywhere. Her mouth did this sort of wobble thing between laughing and crying. Her eyes were clearly in the crying camp, spilling tears unabashedly down her cheeks.

Bryn, who was just behind her, pulled up short like someone had yanked an invisible leash. Then her trademark grin broke across her face, quick and contagious and with just enough edge to make those that knew her nervous.

"Oh of *course* you wake up the one time Fletcher and I convince Ameline to eat her lunch anywhere but in this claustrophobic charmless sick room in an entire week!"

My chest expanded with a gladness so profound only the disgusting sensation in my mouth reassured me that this was not some kind of afterlife.

"My deepest apologies," I said. My voice was rough from disuse. Or had I been screaming? "Want me to pretend to be unconscious again so we can start over?"

Ameline recovered from her shock and flung herself across the room, leaving the shattered glass on the floor in a most uncharacteristic display of wanton disregard for law and order.

Bryn kept her cool and sauntered over, but somehow managed to arrive only a second after Ameline. "That would be great, thanks. We *have* been waiting for this moment for seven whole freaking days."

But there was something I needed to know first. "Did it…? Did we…?" I couldn't get the question out.

"It worked," Bryn confirmed. "The Malus is gone."

A few minutes later, all three of us were squeezed

onto my bed. While I was sure I couldn't smell good, they'd at least brought me a toothbrush so I could brush my teeth with my working arm, which did wonders for making me feel human again. I was too weak to do more. Plus I had too many burning questions I wanted answers for.

I checked Theus to make sure his chest was still rising and falling, then settled more comfortably in between them.

"Tell me everything."

"We pulled it off," Bryn assured me again. "The walkers who sacrificed themselves managed to force the entire core of the Malus into the void."

Even though I had witnessed the beginning of that myself, her words—the full import of them—was hard to take in. Could it really be over?

"We knew it had worked because the rest of the Malus turned into that inert black dust stuff and"—Bryn swallowed hard, her eyes shining—"let's just say I've never been so happy to see the sky."

Ameline nodded vehemently. "Me too. The Echoes lasted a little longer. I guess because they had a semi-distinct life force of their own. But their movements slowed straight away, and within a minute they were too slow to pose much threat. Ten minutes after that, they stopped altogether. It's creepy. There's a whole landscape of monstrous black stone statues now. But Zaltarre thinks it will be good for future generations to have a visual reminder of what happened."

Over. It was really over.

I drew in and released a long slow breath to let that sink in. It felt like I'd been buried alive and the weight of the earth suddenly shifted off me. And even though my whole body was still weak and clumsy and heavy with fatigue, damn me if it didn't feel like I'd been gifted with flight.

Except…

"How many died?" I asked.

Their faces fell.

"In our unit," Bryn said, "we miraculously all made it out alive. In the rest"—she paused, her eyes shuttering for a long, painful moment—"too many."

I accepted that answer. For now it was all I felt strong enough to bear.

And then unbidden, memories of being trapped in stone surfaced. Or had I dreamed that part?

"What about…? How did I survive? I have strange memories of being trapped in Echo stone and knowing Theus wasn't going to get to me in time."

Across the room, Ellbereth stirred, and I used some of her own magic to push her more deeply into sleep.

"You have Gus to thank for that part," Ameline said and wriggled out of our cozy nest to draw him up across my lap.

"We were trying to carve away the stone without, well, carving you. But we wouldn't have gotten to you in time. Gus uh, took matters into his own hands, or he usurped Theus's hands to—well, he did this great overhead swing and nearly completely severed your arm at the shoulder. But it allowed Theus to reach you and shut down your magic."

"Oh, Gus," I purred. "I didn't know you cared."

I merely cannot be bothered teaching some other wielder the art of bathing me. Theus made a right mess of it.

"Better an arm than my life I suppose, but couldn't you have managed to sever my *nondominant* arm?"

Partially *severed,* he corrected. *Ungrateful wench.*

"Helena managed to reattach it just enough that you wouldn't lose the whole thing, and she thinks in time as your life force regenerates, the damage to the nerves and muscles will heal so long as you rest it and avoid lifting anything heavy for three months," Ameline assured me quickly.

Never mind that if Theus hadn't dithered so long trying to cut you out without injury, you might have had enough life force left to heal it properly then and there.

Something clicked in my sluggish brain. "Wait, if Theus was well enough to swing a sword and then bathe Gus afterward, how come he looks close to comatose all these days later?"

Bryn and Ameline exchanged glances.

I felt a twinge of unease.

"That's a longer story," Ameline said. "You didn't

die instantly from the withdrawal backlash of all that power like we feared. But you had a fever so high Helena said it was a wonder your organs weren't already failing. By the time we got you back to the base, you were sweating and thrashing and couldn't keep anything down. And you were getting worse, not better."

Bryn chimed in. "Theus was convinced it was only your bond to Ellbereth's life force that was keeping you alive. But she was in just as bad shape as you. And you were both deteriorating. The healers couldn't do anything because the withdrawal was sapping your combined life energy faster than you could regenerate it."

The strain on their faces as they recounted this gave me some idea of how terrified they'd been. How long had they watched me teeter closer and closer to the edge of death? A week, Bryn had said.

Remembering the misery I'd experienced in those few seconds before they'd burst through the door, I knew their week had been worse than mine.

"Theus was determined to save you," Ameline said quietly. "Well, we all were, but he was the only one who came up with a way to do it. He transported himself to the human cache and bound himself to your life force the same way you'd done with Ellbereth."

"It was gloriously ballsy," Bryn declared in evident admiration. "No one knew whether it would offer enough strength to heal you and Ellbereth, or if it would only drag him into death with you."

Ameline fiddled with the blanket, eyes downcast. "I tried to talk him out of it. I thought that's what you would've wanted."

I reached awkwardly with my left hand to find and squeeze hers. "You're right. I would've tried to talk him out of it too."

Bryn scoffed. "Well he sure as heck wasn't going to listen to either of you. I've never seen him so hell-bent on anything. And he was right. As soon as he bound himself to you, your fever finally went down, your breathing grew less labored, and you fell into a sort of peaceful sleep rather than unconsciousness. That was four days ago."

My eyes darted for about the hundredth time over to Theus's sleeping figure.

He'd risked everything for me.

Again.

I shouldn't have been surprised. He'd always willingly shared my burdens. Yet this time was different. This time the Malus had already been defeated. This time he'd risked eighty years of relative peace rather than a decade of war and the end of our world.

Ameline, Bryn, and I chatted a while more, but fatigue was pulling at me.

"You look awful," Bryn observed.

"She means you look exhausted," Ameline amended. "Why don't you sleep?"

Her worried frown shifted into a smile.

"Now that the Malus no longer threatens us, there'll be plenty of time for talk."

I awoke to familiar voices.

"Yes," Bryn said. "She came to a few hours ago. She wasn't exactly firing at full capacity, but we told her the story of your heroic rescue and even before that her eyes kept drifting to you unwittingly about five times a minute. She was so obvious even Lirielle would've picked it up."

"Ah." This voice was raspy but unmistakably Theus. "Lirielle's known for months. I thought she was being prophetic at first, but she laughed and told me, 'No, it's just *that* obvious.'"

Bryn snickered. "Yes, I'm pretty sure the whole academy and half the army knew before you two did."

"Um." Ameline sounded hesitant. "Griff says Nova's awake... and eavesdropping."

"Is that right?" Theus asked, his tone rich with amusement.

"Guilty," I croaked, opening my eyes to see the four of them. "But nobody likes a tattletale, Griff." I gave the griffin a half-hearted glare. After *all* the tidbits I'd fed him too!

Bryn shot to her feet. "Ohhh, I just remembered

we need to go to that thing." She was about as subtle as one of her fireballs.

"What thing?" Ameline asked, completely missing it.

"You know, the *thing*. That we need to go to. Right now."

Bryn whispered in Ameline's ear.

"Oh right, *that* thing," Ameline said, and the pair of them scampered out the room, Bryn pausing just long enough to give me an exaggerated wink.

At least Griff went with them.

I was pleased to find that I felt strong enough to walk over to Theus. So I did.

I perched on the edge of his bed.

He was sitting propped against the pillows, and his gaze drank me in, even though I doubtless looked as beaten up as he did.

"I heard you found another way to almost die for me," I said, trying to hide my sudden case of nerves. "I don't know whether to thank you or yell at you."

"I vote for the first option."

My lips tugged up, but I quickly sobered again. He was too thin, his freckles dark against his pallid skin. It was impossible to look at him without grasping the enormity of the risk he'd taken and the toll it had exacted in a few short days. How close had he come to dying?

"I can't believe you bound your life to mine," I whispered.

"Yes." His tone was light and teasing. "I'm afraid you're stuck with me now."

I snorted at this supposed hardship. "I wouldn't be so sure. I find extended distances from Ellbereth cause me no trouble."

He frowned, but his eyes laughed at me, and it was all I could do not to kiss him.

But I had things I needed to say with words first.

"Thank you. That was… huge."

He'd already given up so much of his life to become a hollow. Half his natural lifespan. Then he'd faced death again and again to keep me alive and defeat the Malus. And then, just when it was all over, just when he *had* a chance at a future he had some say in, he'd risked it all for me.

"I hope…" I swallowed. "I hope it doesn't end up costing you too many of your remaining years."

Because even with the immediate danger over, now that his life was bound to mine, and mine to Ellbereth's, if any one of us died young, we all would.

Theus reached out and brushed his fingers along my cheek. My thoughts scattered beneath his touch.

"It wasn't as selfless as you're making out," he said. "I'd prefer to live fewer years with you than another eighty alone."

I stared at him. Even gaunt and unwell he was ridiculously beautiful. His deep green eyes stared back with utter sincerity. And the dark shadows under those eyes and his cracked lips were both testament to how much he loved me.

My question came out breathier than I intended. "Who said you'd be alone? Now that humans and walkers are going to intermingle more, I think you'll find many willing partners prepared to throw themselves at your feet. You're very good-looking by human standards, you know."

He chuckled, a soft, low sound deep in his throat. It traveled through my body like sparks. "Oh? Is that so? I might need to reconsider then."

I reached out, hooked my good arm around his neck, and pulled his face to meet mine. "Too late," I informed him.

Then I kissed him. Again.

And it turned out my memory was just as crap as my imagination, because it still blew my expectations out of the water.

CHAPTER THIRTY-THREE

For one day, we celebrated.

Reaper unit sat around a table in the crowded mess hall. Most of our fellow hollows were wearing uniforms still, but not a single soul was on duty.

Valesk looked a little lost without that purpose.

Silvyr sipped his drink and let out a long dramatic sigh. "Well, hell. *Now* what am I going to do? I'm too youthful and brimming with potential to retire."

"I'm not," Helena grumped.

"Better to be brimming with actual skills and experience than potential anyway," Valesk declared.

"Or this berry wine stuff," Dax put in.

Helena took a swig of her own drink. "I think I'd rather just retire."

Orlandrus was evidently musing on grander matters. "Humans used to be wildly enthusiastic about sporting events, didn't they? Do you think we could turn Blob Blast into a worldwide sensation?"

"Ooh, yes," Dax enthused. "Then Bryn could join our team and we could play professionally. My great grandma was a professional hockey player."

"My grandmother was a seer," Lirielle offered absently—as if we weren't all hyperaware of that fact. "But I heard she couldn't tell a sword from a stick."

Xanther said nothing as usual, but he looked more relaxed than I'd ever seen him, his long wiry frame all but draped over his chair.

And Fletcher was different too. He was neither the affable boy next door I'd once adored nor the haunted stranger that had filled my heart with grief every time I saw him. He would never be the same person he once was, and that was okay. Because there was a light in his brown eyes now, and he no longer held himself apart from the people around him. *It's different out here,* he'd told me. *Caring too much is a liability.* But the way his gaze kept flitting to Ameline, I thought he'd overcome that hang-up.

It was good to celebrate. More than good. But we kept the celebration to a single day, because I wasn't alone in wanting to return to my family.

Not that everyone was so keen. There were those like Bryn whose blood relations had treated them poorly. And others who had not seen their families for ten, twenty, or thirty years and were unsure how they would be received. Would they find the figures from their distant but beloved memories still recognizable in the flesh? Or merely strangers who looked familiar?

"You're coming with me," I told Bryn. "I can't wait to introduce you to my little sister. She's only five, but I think she might give you a run for your money."

Bryn's eyes grew bright, but she cocked a hand on her hip. "I was always so envious of *normal* families. Guess it's time to learn whether the grass really is greener on the other side, or I was just delusional."

"Maybe a bit of both," I teased.

Fletcher and Ameline were coming to Los Angeles as well of course. And Theus. Lirielle likewise received an invitation that was more like an order from me. I'd learned her mother died in childbirth and the walker who'd raised her had been among those that had departed for their home world, so she had no one to return to.

We would be accompanied by dozens of older firstborns who'd come from our settlement and survived the intervening years. There would be many tearful, joyous reunions tomorrow.

The reason most of the army was still here to celebrate *with* after my week's convalescence was that everyone was suddenly scrambling to plan for a future that hadn't existed a week ago. No one had worried about human-walker integration, the planet's regeneration, and strategies to deal with the far-reaching aftermath of the Firstborn Agreement when the world was ending.

Now we had to.

It was a good problem to have.

But it was also difficult to address.

Here on the war front, the division between walkers and humans had blurred so far as to become indistinct. Fighting alongside one another for years against a common enemy had forged bonds that the rest of the world would not understand. More specifically, the general human population would not understand.

Most would feel how I did about walkers seven months ago. And explaining the truth behind the Firstborn Agreement wasn't going to go far in altering perceptions, not when the walkers had knowingly released the Malus onto our world.

Yet humans had grown dependent on walker protection and provisions. And a significant portion of the walkers who'd been providing those services had left or were in the process of leaving for their home planet.

Then there was the regeneration. It was estimated seventy percent of the earth had been decimated. The walker's life magic and preservation efforts—especially the Preservatorium where the firstborns who'd failed the initial phase of the academy had been put to work caring for a multitude of endangered flora and fauna species—meant we had hope of undoing some of that damage. Teams were already assembling to begin that massive undertaking. But it would take many, many years.

In the meantime, there was plenty of land and vacant homes to go around. (I already knew which piece I wanted.)

If there was one silver lining to the Lord Brackenfort fiasco, it was that the walkers who had chosen to stay (and the hollows whose choice had been taken from them) were those who cared most about the fate of our world.

It was going to be challenging. But it seemed a more hopeful challenge than facing down the Devourer of worlds. And while it was going to take time—generations probably—to achieve all we wanted to, time was one resource we now had.

So for tonight, we celebrated what we'd achieved so far. Our triumph over darkness.

It was a story that would need to be told everywhere and repeated often. A story of 373 walkers who had courageously sacrificed themselves, feeding their life energy to the Malus. Of the hundreds more humans and walkers alike who had given their lives in that final thrust. Of thousands of strange creatures who'd donated their life's energy to the task. A story of the triumph of human and walkers and creatures working together.

It was a story of the hollows who could not leave and would now call our world home. Of the walker magic that held our decimated planet in balance and offered a future of hope and promise and healing.

It was *not* a story of the prophesied ones. Though that part too would need to be understood to explain just how the walkers had come to choose our world.

Nor was it a pretty story where the villains were punished and the heroes lived happily ever after. Real life wasn't so black and white.

But I sincerely hoped it would be a story that would help our peoples learn what we could from the past, step firmly into the present, and forge a new future together.

CHAPTER THIRTY-FOUR

Theus fidgeted nervously.

The only other time I'd seen him do that was four months ago when discussing my possible execution.

"What will your family think of me?" he asked.

We'd tried to make him and Lirielle a little less stunningly beautiful—a little less identifiably walkers —then given up and made them both wear hooded cloaks even though it was a hot summer's day in Los Angeles.

I smiled up at him where his green eyes were shadowed by the cloak. "Oh, Mom won't like you *at all*. But don't take it personally, she never liked anyone I brought home except for Ameline. And dad will probably threaten retaliation if you dare hurt me, but don't let him fool you. He's a softy under all the hulk. Reuben might actually like having another man in the house. He was always complaining about being outnumbered. But he's thirteen so he might decide he hates you just on principle."

I trailed off, trying not to laugh at his increasingly horrified expression.

"Don't look so appalled. You've already won the rest of my family over." I waved a hand to indicate Bryn, Ameline, Fletcher, and Lirielle.

Theus did not look reassured.

We dropped Ameline and Fletcher off outside their own homes and stepped through a final gateway into the corridor of my old apartment building.

Would my family be home? I couldn't get to the door handle quick enough. It was unlocked, so I pushed through the door into the worn but tidy living area.

We spotted each other at the same time.

Mila had grown at least an inch since I'd last seen her. Her face lit up and she started running, her features split in the most beautiful gap-toothed grin.

I promptly burst into tears.

Her running steps slowed, and I cried harder for ruining this moment for her. But she was only slowing to reach into her pocket.

"Don't cry, Nova," she chirped in her high singsong voice, and she pulled out a grubby hand-kerchief.

That same damn handkerchief I'd given her seven months ago.

It was in sore need of a wash. Or burning. But I

accepted it from her feeling like it was the most precious thing in the world.

I knelt down and hugged her with my good arm. My throat was so tight with joy it hurt. "Thank you."

And then I was airborne as my dad couldn't wait any longer and lifted me in the mother of all bear hugs. "Nova, Nova, Nova," he half sang, half cried, his voice breaking on those two simple syllables of my name. "You came back to us." Tears slid down his rough, stubbled cheeks and onto mine. "I have always and will always love you to the stars and back, but I much prefer to have you home."

So many tears were pouring down my face by that point that I caved and used Mila's filthy handkerchief to wipe some of them away.

Reuben had sidled up while dad was twirling me around. His hair was longer and there was an extra swagger in the way he held himself, but he threw his street cred to the wind and hugged me tight.

For about one point five seconds. "Is that a sword? Can I hold it? Is it sharp? What were the monsters like? Did you kill them?"

My mother's hug was as stiff as I expected, but her eyes scoured my face as if seeing me, truly seeing me, for the first time in years. And I dared to hope that we might begin to build a better relationship now the shadow of the Firstborn Agreement no longer hung over our heads.

The world's problems were far from fixed. Thousands of years of history said they probably never would be. But we were no longer on the brink of extinction. And here in this moment, we were together. Our family complete once more, with a few additional members I'd brought with me.

And we weren't the only ones. For the first time in thirty-seven years, human families everywhere could experience a sense of wholeness. Could hug their firstborns or eldest siblings without fear that tomorrow they would be ripped from their arms. Could experience a day together unclouded by the grief, guilt, fear, and anger surrounding the Firstborn Agreement, free of the heartbreak that had ricocheted through every generation.

Free.

Dad turned to the three figures waiting behind me. Theus, Bryn, and Lirielle.

"And who do we have here?" he asked.

"These are my dear friends who helped me survive and make it home," I said. "How about we put the kettle on and get comfortable? I have a story to tell you."

EPILOGUE

Two months later...

It was the perfect day for a picnic. The sun was shining, a light, fragrant breeze drifted across the sky, and the lake sparkled in the dappled afternoon light. And since our lives had settled into a kind of glorious normalcy, we did exactly that.

We laid out blankets on Millicent's pristine lawn, ate and drank until our stomachs were content, and soaked up the sunshine.

It had taken little convincing to persuade my family to eschew the old dingy apartment in Los Angeles for the grand splendor of Millicent Manor.

Well, actually, Mom had complained about all the work it would take to move and how she didn't trust those hedge cats to protect us and why on earth did the building need our blood anyway—until she'd experienced the wonder of a hot shower.

She didn't exactly thank me after that, but she packed everyone's things real quick.

Ameline, Fletcher, and Griff had stayed with their own families and the rest of the community in Los Angeles. But with multiple walkers around and my access to Ellbereth's magic, it was easy to travel back and forth. In fact, since we had rooms permanently set aside for them and they visited with such regularity, it might be fairer to say they half lived with us.

Millicent had seemed just as happy with the arrangement as I was. Although the first time I showered, she pranked me with icy water for two horrifying seconds. She also insisted on drawing blood every time we entered one of the bedrooms, confirming my long-held suspicion that it wasn't *just* for security. Still, it was a small enough price to pay.

To my surprise, Glenn and Glennys had stayed on as well. Apparently they'd grown more attached to Millicent than their walker rescuers.

They had given Mom a fright, but Mila loved them. And I could've sworn I saw *Glenn* sneaking her an extra serving of cake after dinner the other night and smiling broadly to cover it up.

The golin version of a smile had *also* given Mom a fright.

Mila had Ameline's charm and Bryn's penchant for

mischief, and every day I watched with a mixture of terror and delight to see what she'd get up to next. Yesterday she'd had one of the giant hedge cats following her around the garden like an oversized kitten. The day before that she'd found the old wand case in Professor Grimwort's class (why the heck hadn't they taken those things with them?) and set one of the chandeliers on fire.

There were painful memories as well as good ones. I visited Cricklewood's office and cried despite myself. But I was confident that as time went on and we made more and more memories, the good ones would outweigh the bad.

Reuben adored swimming in the lake and rather liked the various weapon caches too. I hadn't managed to bring myself to join him in the water yet, but Theus obliged him most days. Judging by the light in Reuben's eyes, that might have been better anyway. His street cred had gone through the roof once he started inviting his friends to spend the summer with him.

There was plenty of room for everyone.

Which was another wonderful thing about living here. We'd opened Millicent's doors to anyone who had nowhere else to call home.

Most veterans, walker and human alike, had found agreeable options for occupation and lodging. Even those estranged from or abandoned by their families.

Every day, more people joined the regeneration efforts and relieved those who wished to leave the Preservatorium. Others, including some of the more charismatic walkers, visited human settlements to strengthen their protections and assist with any other needs to begin the mammoth task of generating goodwill. (Valesk had wisely chosen a course that *wouldn't* require charisma.) But some souls yearned for something different.

Xanther had moved in with us. After nearly a quarter of a century of war, he wanted peace and quiet far away from the barren lands. It turned out he had a green thumb even by walker standards and was teaching Mom and Dad how to set up a self-sufficient garden. Sometimes he even deigned to use words.

Helena came too. Heaven knows she'd earned her retirement. Although between Mila's mischief and Reuben and his friends' fascination with weapons, she seemed to have someone to patch up on a near daily basis. At least Mom and Dad were appreciative of her presence.

Silvyr, Dax, and Orlandrus had taken up fancy pants lodgings in the walker city, but they visited us sometimes. They and Bryn were determinedly inflicting Blob Blast on the newest generation. I stuck with my vow to avoid the game, but Reuben and his friends thought it was pretty great, and Mila adored it. She'd never been grubbier. Or happier.

As a result, Theus had become adept at magicking

handkerchiefs out of thin air. A useful trick even Mom admired. Except he told me secretly he'd made a small gateway into the linen closet and just made sure to replenish them frequently.

Lirielle split her time between us and the team working with the Preservatorium. Somehow she always knew exactly where a protected species would thrive when being reintroduced into the wild.

Ellbereth—to no one's surprise—stayed in the walker city and wrote nasty notes sent by skyfury every time I used her magic. The skyfury was super cute, and sometimes I used magic just to see the little critter.

After a leisurely group picnic in the sun, Theus and I stole away for some alone time.

Dad wasn't happy about us walking around unchaperoned, but I'd argued that if I was old enough to have paid the price of the firstborn, faced down death, and helped defeat the worst monster the worlds had ever seen, I was surely old enough to be alone with a boy. Even one as handsome as Theus.

Or was that *especially* one as handsome as Theus?

To my surprise, Mom had sided with me.

Theus and I went to one of our favorite rooms, which had a particularly nice view and a particularly comfy couch, and sank down into the latter.

I took his hand in mine, reveling in its familiarity. But there was something that had been bugging me lately. Something that seemed more and more unfair the happier I felt.

"You know," I murmured, "so many of my hopes have been realized, and yet despite every impossible thing we've managed to pull off, we didn't really fix anything for you. You'll still only live half your natural lifespan. You're still stuck on this world, never able to experience the thing you were made for. I'm sorry—"

"I'm not." He trailed kisses along my jawline, as if to emphasize his point. "I could have walked the worlds for every one of my two hundred years and never found you. That would've been far too steep a price." He kissed me again, his lips soft but sure against mine.

I kissed him back, smiling, but then pulled away a fraction. "That's all very sweet, but you don't have to sugarcoat the truth for me. Not ever. I remember the yearning on your face when you spoke of the freedom of walking between worlds. You said you were *made* for it."

His dark green eyes met mine, intently serious. "You know what I realized recently?"

"What?"

"Even the most adventuresome world walkers always return. No matter how many worlds they visit, no matter how many wonders they see, they always come home."

He raked his gaze over my face, lingering on my lips before meeting my eyes again. "I didn't understand that, but now I think I do. And Nova, in you I've found my home."

Then he kissed me again with sultry intensity and drew me closer.

This time I didn't even think about pulling away.

Millicent locked the door with an audible click.

DID YOU MISS LEARNING GUS'S
CENTURIES-OLD SECRET?

FIND OUT IN THIS FUN AND FAST
BONUS SCENE!

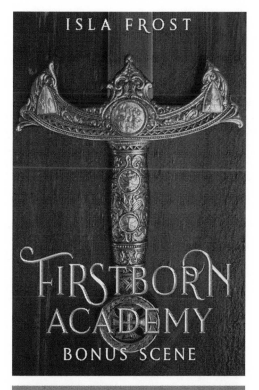

FOR ALL BOOKS BY THIS AUTHOR,
PLEASE VISIT:

ISLAFROST.COM

ABOUT THE AUTHOR

Isla Frost is the pen name of a bestselling mystery author whose first love has always been fantasy. She loves to write about strong heroines in fast-paced stories full of danger, magic, and adventure that leave you feeling warm and satisfied.

She also loves apple pie.

Be the first to hear about new releases and get exclusive bonus content by signing up at www.islafrost.com

Made in the USA
Monee, IL
16 January 2020